My  Heart

Patricia Burgess-McCormick

Published by

Forward Thinking Publishing

Copyright © 2022 by Patricia Burgess-McCormick

All rights reserved. No part of this publication may be reproduced, distributed or transmitted in any form or by any means, including photocopying, recording, or other electronic or mechanical methods, without the prior written permission of the publisher and/or author, except in the case of brief quotations embodied in critical reviews and certain other noncommercial uses permitted by copyright law.

All events and people have been fictionalised.

A catalogue record for this book is available from the British Library.

ISBN: 978-1-8380445-9-6

Contents

Part 1

Chapter 1 1

Chapter 2 4

Chapter 3 9

Chapter 4 12

Chapter 5 19

Chapter 6 24

Chapter 7 29

Chapter 8 34

Chapter 9 37

Chapter 10 43

Chapter 11 45

Chapter 12 51

Chapter 13 57

Chapter 14 61

Chapter 15 67

Chapter 16 70

Chapter 17 74

Part 2

Chapter 18 79

Chapter 19 84

Chapter 20 86

Chapter 21 92

Chapter 22 97

Chapter 23 102

Chapter 24 106

Chapter 25 113

Chapter 26 117

Chapter 27 121

Chapter 28 129

Chapter 29 133

Chapter 30 139

Chapter 31 141

Chapter 32 149

Chapter 33 158

Chapter 34 161

Chapter 35 171

Chapter 36 181

About the Author 189

For Giovanna and Michela

'Deep assignments run through all our lives; there are no coincidences.'

—J.G. Ballard

PART 1

Chapter 1

I am of Ireland,

And of the holy land

Of Ireland.

Good sir, pray I thee,

For of saint charity,

Come dance with me

In Ireland.

(Anonymous Medieval Irish Lyric)

IRELAND. I AM OF Ireland. I have thought of it often, drumming up images of it while standing in London, Paris, Luxembourg, Milan, Alsace, or Rome. I carried moving pictures of it in my stupid, stubborn, and sentimental Irish soul. Above all, I pictured her shores, her shores which I have watched recede many more times than I ever wished, or ever thought would be necessary, and the strings of my heart tightening as the distance between us increased. "Ah, don't worry, it'll still be there when you get back," said an old man up on deck, observing my distress, recognising it.

Would it? Instinct is no fool. I knew it would be different. Like the precious baby you leave with strangers for a week. When you return with love in your heart, your child wears a different face, the face that someone else has given it in your absence, and holds you at arm's length, not forgiving you for leaving it, and you ache because time has been lost, and is irretrievable.

But there is always the returning. I know well the feeling of rapture as Dun Laoghaire comes into view. Remember the early days. Sailing into the harbour, into my future, the freezing wind in my face and my heart, my young girl's heart, as it was then, breaking with joy to be back and all the good things in store! Watching the land approach – my God, what hopes I had! What madness!

> *That is no country for old men. The young*
>
> *In one another's arms,*
>
> *birds in the trees*
>
> *Those dying generations*
>
> *(W.B. Yeats)*

At college we were fond of Yeats. In my case, he was particularly close to the heart. Like myself, Yeats was a victim of his own particular vision of Ireland. He understood love. Especially the unrequited, unconsummated kind.

Where does love come from? We know nothing of its beginnings. One day it flutters, like a baby quickening inside the womb, and we are aware of it for the first time. In that moment of recognition a lightning decision is taken, a gut reaction, to be or not to be – to give the go-ahead or deny. But who can resist the roller coaster of love? Virgins cannot be wise. And no one believes that their ending will not be happy.

Chapter 2

MY FIRST LOVE WAS a very Irish man. His voice was an invitation to the dance. It promised all the things I had dreamed about. He invited love he did not know how to accept, love he had no use for.

As time unfolded, I began to see that he did not know any more than me what was to be done with it. Then I had a crisis. The preliminary steps in this treacherous dance were spell binding, irresistible. I held back slightly but I was dumb, incapable of argument. It is not hyperbole to say I worshipped the ground he walked on. When I chanced to catch sight of him along Nassau Street or O'Connell Bridge, it seemed as though my heart rushed up to meet my throat. I loved him even more for the feelings he inspired in me. Is this a foretaste of the divine? In any case, it can quickly become a religion.

What days those were! Striding out every morning in my health and youth. Never having encountered defeat I ignored that it existed. Swanning through the city I loved, the morning air all around me, I felt like a queen. All good things would come to me as sure as the currents of the Liffey.

Every city has its smells. Dublin smells of her brewery, her famed coffee houses, her river, and the sea at her elbow. There is magic in her air that can make you drunk in conjunction with her strange light.

But ugliness was always there, lurking, the malevolent relative at the christening party. My love was acted out with strange backdrops. In Dublin, much of life takes place in pubs. People take refuge in pubs, from rain, from disappointment, boredom, and from themselves.

They hide in the comforting dusk of the snug, with morning sun filtering through the thick glass of the window panes onto the dark little tables, with their drinks. People talk in pubs. They say things they mean and a lot of things that mean nothing. They sip pints in the quiet of the morning. Time flows painlessly till the barbarity of the Holy Hour when everyone is flung out on the streets, blinking. Then back inside. Oh the growing heartiness of the evening. Listen in on the gossip and bitching, the verbal canoodling and codswallop, the baloney and the pantomime! People confide in pubs, they also destroy one another. Many a vicious battle has been fought over a glass, many a heart broken.

Many of our meetings were in places like this. Realising the gravity of my situation he attempted, far too late, to be honest, responsible. "I am a sick man", he told me. "A very sick man." But I did not believe him. I thought he was all-knowing, in control.

He would talk and I would listen. The love I had so unwisely borne him sat between us like a very beautiful but demented child.

Sometimes the sight of it would incite him to violent speech. The vileness of his words were shots to my core. I grew numb. Like a placatory wife, I sought to hide my offspring lest it incite the wrath of he who had fathered it. It should never have been born. There was something unwholesome in it. We were both ashamed of the freak we had produced and terrified that people would notice it and talk. And yet, despite my shame, I held its hand quietly, defiantly, hoping that in time, with patience, it would somehow be transformed into something acceptable.

After many months he took me to his bed. We both lay down in our boots, and catching sight of my feet, he complained about their size. Being of that generation of men who believe in their souls that women should be dainty, my wildness at once drew him and repelled him.

I was prepared for abnormality. Everything in our relationship had conformed to it thus far, I knew it was unlikely to change. I had hoped for passion as he took me in his arms and gently kissed my forehead. Words of love? He proceeded to tell me about the life of Shakespeare, adding "...he never moves me, Shakespeare, I dunno, he never moves me..."

In desperation I confronted him with the insanity of my aspirations, he was perturbed, but resolutely denied their validity. My head spun with the sickness of rejection. I left in confusion and found myself, drunk with pain, back in my flat, where concerned friends tried in vain to understand, console, and reason.

How can I describe the death of my bird of love? With finally fluttering wings it strove to annihilate itself, and I gasped, transformed by a disappointment so huge it threatened life itself. The world was powerless to help. There was no sense anywhere. It seemed as though I could never again want anything so badly as the love of this sick, middle-aged man, with his crazy, wonderful visions and his cruelty.....

Love is a powerful drug. To wean herself off it, the addict must undergo withdrawal pains of the most searing kind. Now I walked Dublin's streets with very different steps. I was saturated with grief. My face aged with the tears my eyes wept, I prayed, I blasphemed, I cursed and ranted. And then the little love bird I had cherished for so long grew still and sullen as it recognised its end.

Hate and anger suffused me. My sadness poisoned everything. Where once I had seen beauty, now I saw only muck and ugliness. The futility of life filled me with fury until at last, I grew apathetic, despairing. How long the days were then. How to fill them? I began to pray then, for deliverance from the life-sapping indifference which was destroying my soul. I deliberately sought pain as a welcome alternative to the deadness I carried inside me.

Chapter 3

WHEN WE WERE KIDS and we drove from County Tyrone to Dublin, everyone was in a good mood. The journey was long, but no one minded, and we would sing as the car rolled along:

"And we're all off to Dublin in the green, in the green,

Where the helmets glisten in the sun,

Where the bayonets flash and the rifles crash

To the rattle of a Thompson gun."

("Off to Dublin in the green" by The Dubliners)

My sister Margaret and I would doze off, and then hours later, my mother would prod us awake.

"Wake up, wake up! We're here, we're in Dublin!"

My mum was as excited as we were. She had been born and reared in Dublin and her beloved mother still lived here.

I remember opening my eyes and there were cars everywhere. We were in a huge wide street, and we drove past O'Connell's big grey statue, with the beautiful big angels at its foot. I wished the car window was rolled down so that I could reach out and touch their wings. I knew we were in the heart of Dublin and not far from my grandmother's house.

My sister and I got excited and so we bounced up and down on the car seat until our father told us to keep still. When we got to Nana's house we ran inside – very excited to see everyone. Two of my mother's brothers were there with Nana in the kitchen, waiting to see us all; Uncle Michael and Uncle Gil, and they laughed as Margaret and I ran in calling out. "Will you listen to the wee Northerners!" they said, teasing us about our Northern Irish accents.

Everything was better because we were in Dublin. It was as though a weight had been lifted. The streets were wider, the buildings were bigger, and the air was freer. I loved the Liffey, the smell of it, and the smell of the Guinness hops that lingered everywhere.

Now after years and years of wishing and planning, my dream has come true.

Chapter 4

I AM AN UNDERGRADUATE at the famous Trinity College, in the centre of my beloved city. Sometimes I can hardly believe my luck.

I am on my way to a lecture. I rush down Merrion Square and into Nassau Street, past the Kilkenny Design, and then cross over to the Trinity Railings. Chattering groups of students block my path as they wait for buses but they make way for me good-naturedly, and very soon I turn right, past the tall tree at the Arts Block entrance – into beautiful Trinity College, where I am so proud to be an undergraduate.

The hum of energy which characterises the Arts Block is a bit like the swarm of bees. It ebbs and flows, but it goes on all day long. This is where the young and beautiful come to pose and gossip. The girls dress up and lounge back holding their polystyrene coffee cups, or they stand, for better effect. The fellows are taut and talkative. Everyone is looking at each other, taking in the scene, sizing up the talent. Appointments are made here, "see you after the Yeats lecture?" "Have you written that essay yet – the Duchess of Malfi one?" "What options are you going for next semester? American literature or Modernist Poets?" People fall in and out of love over the big square blocks that take the place of seats in this hall.

I push my way through the chattering crowd, casting a hurried eye over the animated figures. I was unlikely to see any of my friends at this ungodly hour. I continue up the stairs to my lecture.

The lecture will be given by the so-called Divine Miss Sally Kane: tall, elegant, blonde, and very brainy. Thereby hung a tale – for Sally Kane had been married to Professor Kielty, and though now separated, their union still reverberated through the college.

Dr Kane had already begun her lecture, so I slid quietly into my seat and prepared to concentrate very hard as her lectures on the dialectic of American literature were always difficult for me to follow.

I found it impossible to concentrate while she delivered her impeccably crafted lecture on Nathaniel Hawthorne and his Scarlet Letter. Secretly I had been baffled and dismayed to find that same sexual paranoia and guilt in this seminal piece of American literature that I only thought could be found in Irish culture. I found it difficult and depressing to think about.

Afterwards, I hurried down the little corridor to Kielty's office, my heart pounding. I really needed to see him. For several months now, I had been in love with my Professor, Desmond Kielty. Thoughts of him fill me all day, I long to see him. I tap at the door – no answer. I decide to try his rooms. Professor Kielty lives on campus.

Back down the Arts Block stairs, with a cursory glance at the noticeboard, out into the weak sunshine, over to Front Square and devilish little cobbles! How many heels have been wrecked on these infernal little stones? Past the Campanile towards New Square and up the stairs to Kielty's rooms.

His rooms are at the top. Out of breath, I tap on the door. Again, no answer. Disappointed, I turn to retrace my steps. I decide it's time for some tea so I cross New Square again, carefully, (because I can't afford to get my shoes re-heeled again) and down Front Square, past the sacred Players' noticeboard and exiting Trinity's main entrance, into College Green and right over O'Connell Bridge. The width and space of O'Connell Street combined with the tangy smell of the Liffey, and the heavy overlay of Guinness' hops lifts my spirits as it never fails to do.

There are two Bewley's; one in Grafton Street and one in Westmoreland Street. For my money, the one in Westmoreland Street wins hands down. I stride out past The Liberator on his massive pedestal, surrounded by all his glorious angels, and enter in search of the comfort of Bewley's.

Inside, Bewley's is the heady mix of coffee beans from so many different places. I haven't eaten yet, and the wonderful smell makes me light-headed. It is like a vast temple with heady smells and exotic colours. I slip through to the main café area and queue up quickly for my little tea-pot of tea (proper tea leaves – no such thing as a teabag in here) and a currant bun.

I take a pew on one of the lovely red velvet high-backed seats and take off my coat. For a moment I sit back and relax, waiting for the tea to brew. I love this place, with its waitresses in their old-fashioned white blouses and aprons and their neat black skirts. There are exotic drawings on the coloured glass windows, and ornate, romantic, faded wallpaper.

I notice that someone has left their Irish Times behind them on the bench next to me, and I happily unfold it, to read the headlines. The gruesome story of the Kerry Babies is front page again. For a moment my mind is forced to think beyond the happy confines of Trinity, beyond our happy playground, to the rest of Ireland, to the hidden little communities of the hinterland, where sex is still a dirty word, where ignorance and piety and incest exist.

I sip my tea and cast my eye over the front page. Garret Fitzgerald presides as usual. But I can't concentrate anyway, I am wondering where Kielty is this morning, and how long it will be before I can catch up with him.

Then a familiar figure slides into the seat opposite mine. Philip Conway, an extraordinary young man from Belfast, small, with an almost pretty face – pale skin and small regular features. A few whiskers round his mouth and chin give him an impish air. He is shuffling a pack of cards and muttering to himself.

"What are you up to?" I ask him.

"The cards are Tarot," he replies. "I'm learning to read them. I consult them on all important matters. They help me to make decisions, decide on a course of action etc."

Already a prolific short story writer, Philip is currently obsessed with theatre and has begun devising his own school of drama. He begins to expound on his plans as the April sunshine plays out patterns over the dark wood of the table and worn red velvet benches of Bewley's.

"It's going to be called 'The Theatre of the Absurd' he enthuses. His voice is low and nearly always has a hushed kind of excitement in it, his Belfast accent something of a surprise.

I ask him to explain what he means. "Well, it's going to highlight people with special needs, or mental problems – the whole point being – to show 'normal' people that they are not as 'normal' as they think – what is 'normal' anyway?... I want to shock people."

"But why?" Philip looks up from his cards, surprised. Surely the desire to shock is a worthwhile cause in itself?

Then we get down to discussing the play he is about to direct. He has chosen me and Mariam and another girl to play the leads. It is a short drama based on the poem 'Three Women' by Sylvia Plath. We have already spent a weekend painting the inside of Players Theatre white, to try and make it look like the inside of a hospital.

"Look, I'm meeting Mariam at Front Gate now because it's almost time for rehearsal. Let's go," I say. Philip nods enthusiastically. Like many people, he is a great fan of Mariam's.

Mariam is waiting for us at Front Gate. Together we pass into the echoing porch and talk excitedly about our venture. We bump into Kielty who is on his way out. We urge him to come and see us in our play. He rolls his comical eyes at us, "What's it called?"

"Three Women", says Philip importantly. "It's an adaptation of a Plath poem."

"Three Women?" says Kielty. "Sure one's enough!"

We laugh. We know he will never attend. He will never align himself too closely with any student activity, he likes to keep himself slightly apart. Philip is scathing. "Sure, that man is only interested in seeing a play if it's one of his own!"

Professor Kielty goes on his way and I am chagrined that I have not been able to slide away with him. I stay listening to Philip. We will be dressed in white gowns to look like women on a maternity ward. It's going to be amazing.

Chapter 5

JUST AS WELL I was into Players and acting because I found out I was not really an academic.

At college, they introduced us to a tough programme of disillusionment. The enjoyment of literature became an abstraction as they plunged us headlong into the deadly discipline of criticism and analysis. As time went on, I squirmed with something akin to pain as I watched poems subjected to vivisection. The lecturers got out their academic scalpels and carved away until they destroyed the heart of the literature. I began to feel alienated from much of my course.

My studies began to bore me. They gave us huge, long ponderous novels to read, like 'Pamela'. We used them as door props and went to cafes, pubs, or each other's digs for fun and entertainment.

I began to feel that much of the course was obsolete for me. So I read on my own and joined societies and clubs to fill the time. It never occurred to me to quit my studies, although I was finding them unsatisfying, for somehow a degree was expected of me. Anyway, it provided me with a valid reason for staying on in Dublin.

In my first year, I shared a house in Monkstown with Siobhan. A big old Georgian house overlooking Dublin Bay. It had glorious high ceilings and was filled with old books on everything from ancient Greece to modern German politics. Siobhan's family were all scholars and previous generations had deposited books on various specialist subjects. There were abandoned books in practically every room, even old Latin primers stacked up in the bathroom. You can imagine how much had been amassed over the years.

Siobhan and I amassed nothing. With no grants, and tuition fees to be paid, we eked out an existence on what our parents could afford to send us. In the winter, we froze in the huge unheated rooms. It never occurred to us to use the central heating as we couldn't have covered the bills. Sometimes, to escape the cold, we took refuge in the small kitchen and lit the gas stove, leaving the oven door open and huddling around it drinking hot tea.

Siobhan knew how to make two things; yoghurt, and noodle soup, and she lived on these two staples. She was a clever, lazy girl, with a sense of humour and an easy-going outlook on life. We got on well, but we had different interests and different sets of friends.

I enter the hallway of the house on Trafalgar Terrace. The perfume of ripe apples surrounds me. The house seems quiet, although I can hear birdsong from the back garden to which Siobhan and I do not have any access. I hope my housemate is in.

"Siobhan!" I call out in the wide hall. "Siobhan, are you home?"

There is a pause and then a little thud. Siobhan appears at the top of the stairs.

"Yes, I'm home, ... do you want tea?" She knows the answer. I go up the stairs and follow her into the kitchen, pulling out one of the chairs and sitting down at the battered wooden table where we have spent so many hours talking, analysing, and confiding.

"Your dad rang."

I say nothing to this. Truth is, my English father did not want me to come to Dublin, or study at Trinity. He had a fit when I got my place here. I have always done well at school and dad has high hopes for me. Now I have escaped to Dublin he rings sometimes for news. I feel a pang of guilt about all this because the course I wanted to do would only have taken three years in a British university. Here at Trinity my arts degree will take four long years.

Siobhan has finished making the tea now. She places the little brown pot on the table between us and pushes the milk jug and sugar bowl a little towards me.

"He rings a lot, doesn't he, your dad?" She places a little cube of brown sugar in her mouth and looks at me with raised eyebrows. I am pouring my tea, but I look up at her. She has a cute, shrewd little face, with freckles and glasses. She hasn't been out anywhere today by the look of her, for her hair is unbrushed and she is wearing her comfy, slobbing about clothes; a large unfitted man's shirt, and a saggy skirt of nondescript green.

I don't want to discuss my father with her. "Well, you know," I say conversationally, "He's probably bored. Hertfordshire is a very dull place."

Siobhan looks at me with interest. Although English herself, she has never been there. Her English parents raised her in Hong Kong. She listens to The World Service in her big draughty bedroom, but to her England is an unknown world, as exotic and distant as Hong Kong is to me. To Siobhan, England means romance and Brideshead Revisited, Chariots of Fire, Nigel Havers, Jeremy Irons, and all that. I cannot convey to her the dullness of my life there. The routine, the isolation, the dreary conformity of my school life. I just don't want to talk about it. We exchange anecdotes about our day until she grows bored. She drifts back upstairs and in a few minutes, the house is full of the lovely sound of her flute. She will play for an hour or so now.

She is good enough to be in an orchestra, but she does not have the inclination. In her way, she is a rebel as well. She too has an English father. He bobs up now and again in our conversations; another distant authority figure. She was scornful of my love of Kielty, and I preferred not to confide too much in her.

Chapter 6

THAT SUNDAY MORNING, WHERE was I off to? Somewhere, nowhere. Perhaps the sun had woken me and I had risen, restless to meet another glorious day. The beautiful streets of Dublin opened up before me as I marched along Merrion Square in the welcome early summer sunshine.

In Ireland, May is the summer month – a glorious sunny explosion – usually followed by a damp June and soggy July. But when the sun is shining, it is impossible to imagine it ever stopping. As I walked along I inhaled the hop-tinged air of my beloved city with pleasure. I simply never grew tired of living here. I was nearing Nassau Street now, and the tall railings of Trinity. The streets were uncharacteristically quiet. Past Greene's Bookshop now – the row of posters usually on view by the front door were not there today. Anyway, I knew them all off by heart. I had two favourites; James Joyce cheekily stylish in a jaunty cap and worn-out tennis shoes, and Michael Collins, huge and magnificent in his army uniform, striding out to inspect the troops.

I crossed the road and walked on, past the Nassau Street Arts Block entrance, closed today, and round the corner to College Green and Trinity Front Gate, past Burke and Grattan on their huge pedestals, and on towards O'Connell Bridge. I slowed down now because my unacknowledged wish had come true. Bumbling towards me came Kielty. He beamed when he saw me, and stopped to talk. Love is blind, but even I could see that he was dusty and dishevelled. Perhaps he had not been to bed that night? His wavy hair lay lank and damp on his big skull, frizzy bits around his temples.

"Where are you going?"

"I'm off to get a drink."

"But it's too early. Sure nowhere is open now."

He snorted at me, as if I were an amateur.

"Of course, there's always a drink. If you know where to look. Come with me, Burdey."

I was only too glad to accompany him, but I did wish he would call me by my name instead of 'Burdey'. It wasn't very romantic.

Together we crossed O'Connell Bridge in the sunshine, Kielty sidling down the Quays, looking for the right place. A quick look out for any lurking garda, and then he stands with his back to a dusty shutter and taps quietly on the shut window. Nothing. He taps again. The blind gets hocked up an inch and a minute later the nearby door opens, and a voice exits:

"Is it yourself Kielty? For God's sake, come in!"

They shake hands briefly and next thing, we're in. My eyes are confused for a few moments, for it is dark in here, a contrast to the bright morning outside. Then to the bar. Kielty chatting, smiling, joking, hands over the money gives me my half-pint of Guinness, and downs his Jameson's gratefully in one quick thirsty gulp. Wump. Down the hatch. As if it were medicine. God, but it's dark in here. Almost as dark as a confessional. I remember it's Sunday. We should really be at mass. But I never go now that I'm at college. It's not that I don't believe, it's just too much of an effort to get up and find a mass before midday.

This is how Kielty likes to drink: a creamy pint of Guinness, then a chaser of whiskey, then another pint. Repeat. His blue eyes are bright as he talks to the other men. Few women in here. He looks slightly feverish.

"Who's this here, Kielty?"

Someone nods briefly in my direction. It isn't so much a compliment as a request for confirmation of my credentials.

"She's a friend of mine," he says. "Her name is Burdey, and she's half English and half Irish. I'm trying to work out which half is which."

It's a novelty to be drinking in this illicit hidey-hole with him but after an hour or so I get bored as no one really talks to me. Kielty stands, in his baggy brown trousers and worn-out blue suit jacket, exchanging banter and quips with acquaintances on their way to and from the bar. We come out after a while. Blinking in the sunlight after the dark secret interior of the bar.

We cross over to the river wall, and I lean over and look down at the Liffey. The current is quite fast, the water is alive and sparkling this morning. It is gleaming and beautiful.

"Is it true there are salmon in it?" I ask Kielty.

"Yes," he says, and then he adds "..and mermaids too."

He laughs and his dimples show and his eyes twinkle. I was afraid his mood had darkened after the drinks in the illicit fug, but he is okay. I glance to my left, taking in the imposing Court House, and then to my right, where the shiny tin arc of the Ha'penny Bridge glints like silver this morning. There is nothing more to wish for on a morning like this; the pale sunlight, being here in this city, my most favourite place on earth, standing next to this strange and wonderful man.

Chapter 7

THE DAY THEY SOLD the tickets for the Trinity Ball all the students queued for hours to buy them. A few cynical souls queued in the sun and bought tickets in order to flog them later for twice the price. Advertisements appeared in the Irish Times offering substantial amounts for ball tickets. It was wild. We all looked forward to it like mad. It was all we talked about for weeks.

Of course, getting something good enough to wear was a major concern. Daphne, being clever with the needle, knocked up an outfit for herself, and Siobhan found an old silk dress in one of the presses upstairs in Trafalgar Terrace. Angela hired a gorgeous red velvet number. It was cut low and had a lovely full skirt. It set off her dark hair and creamy skin. She had the loveliest face, soft and heart-shaped, but her parents were divorced and she was hard-hearted about love. She seemed to despise men and was cold to them.

She brought me home and her mother let me look through her wardrobe to see if I could find anything. Most of the dresses were dire; floral monstrosities from the seventies, but at last, we found it; a pale butter-coloured satin dress, Regency style, with a high waist and square, low-cut neckline. It was perfect. I heaved a sigh of relief. All I needed now was my Prince.

We dieted like mad all the week leading up to the big night. Daphne even went to bed for a day to stop herself from getting hungry. A flat stomach was paramount. Another friend, Clare, was making her own dress and worked furiously on it right up to the day.

The night of the ball arrived. I can't remember that much. Just the painful anticipation of it. I went with Angela and two blokes that her mother had drummed up for us. They were the sons of families she knew. Angela's mother was like that – a great one for social networking and engineering.

Angela's beau was good looking. Mine was plump with short red hair. We sat next to each other in the back of the black car that would drive us through Front Gate. He laid a plump hand on my satin-clad knee and squeezed it through the material. I was determined to lose him as soon as we got inside.

The ball wasn't what I had expected. There were no waltzes, no fairy tale candles, no Strauss or romance. There were lots of marquees spread around the grounds, each one housed a different pop band. Someone said there were strawberries and cream so we queued up, but when I got mine I was disappointed that they came in plastic containers. When people had finished they just dropped them on the ground. I wandered about, bumping into different groups of acquaintances. I couldn't see Mariam anywhere.

The hours wore on and I had had quite a lot to drink. I was thirsty now and had a headache. It began to rain and I walked carefully along, holding my cream satin dress up so that the hem would not get soiled. Looking about me, I noted that other girls were not so careful. They stood about now like wilting flowers in their expensive, coloured ball gowns. The hems were dirty and torn from the night's action. Their faces were tired and vacant looking. Perhaps they too had expected something more than this.

At last, I met a bunch of second-year law students I vaguely knew. Aidan invited me to come to their rooms as they were going to have breakfast. A pale pink sky announced that dawn was coming. I clambered up the stairs after Aidan and his girlfriend and heard him exclaim in surprise as he tripped over a couple who were lying prostrate at the top of one of the landings. "Jesus!" he muttered in a shocked voice. A minute later I understood why. The couple were having sex. As I walked past them I looked down with curiosity. The girl was lying on her back while her partner grunted around in her beautiful ballgown. Her face was expressionless and her eyes glazed. I realised she was probably very drunk. I hurried past, feeling bad for her. It was all a far cry from Brideshead.

In Aidan's rooms, however, things were more cheerful. Someone put on some jazz and breakfast was served. Thick brown bread with smoked salmon and lashings of Irish whiskey. Some people, it seemed, still remembered how things should be done. I ate heartily, as I was very hungry but the whiskey and the greasy salmon were too much for my empty stomach. I quickly excused myself and escaped to the bathroom where I threw up, retching. Afterwards, I washed my face and examined my appearance in the mirror. My mascara had run a bit, and my face was pale. For no reason, I began to cry quietly into the sink.

The next day we all met up for a post mortem. Only Siobhan said she had really enjoyed herself. Daphne chain-smoked and looked tragic. Her evening had ended badly because her escort was too stingy to get them a cab back to Monkstown at 3 o'clock in the morning when they both felt ready to go home. Instead, he had suggested that they wait for the buses to start up at 4. Daphne, surprised by his meanness, pointed out that it was raining and they would get soaked. Undeterred, her beau suggested that they take shelter in a nearby phone box. So they squeezed in, Daphne crushing her precious silk gown, and stood for over an hour till the number seven bus appeared. Daphne refused to speak to him, maintaining a stoney silence. Even now, the ignominy of the night sat on her. "I never want to see him again," she said.

I agreed that the night had not lived up to expectations.

Monica entertained us with her version of events. She had spent the week leading up to the ball making a fantastic ball gown. We had all been amazed when she showed it to us. She fasted all day so that she would be able to get into it and then overdid the pre-ball champagne and fell fast asleep before she and her friends got out of rooms. She only woke up at three in the morning and managed to get an hour's dancing in before it all ended and she left and went to the Pink Bicycle for breakfast.

Chapter 8

It is the end of May now, and the end of the academic year at Trinity. I am growing anxious and consult my diary frequently, for my days are numbered. Soon I will have to return to my parents' home in Hertfordshire for the long summer break. I have not succeeded in obtaining any summer work. Other students have organised work visas and are going to America until October. I am dreading the end of Trinity term. I know that my life back in England will be nothing but a boring waste of time, as it was before I came to Dublin.

My journey back to the UK is all planned and paid for. I will get the ferry from Dun Laoghaire to Holyhead, and then the endless train journey from Holyhead, through north Wales and then through England down to Victoria. From there I will get the train to Stevenage. Even then my journey will not be over. My parents, who have always liked to live as far away from the action as possible, live in a tiny village which has no trains or bus services. My father will pick me up from the station in his car.

It doesn't take long for me to clear out of the little box room at the top of Siobhan's house in Monkstown. I only have a few clothes and books and essays to take with me. I don't much care about any of it. I bundle everything carelessly into two big holdalls and quit Ireland with a heavy heart.

When I get home I can't stop thinking and talking about my life in Trinity. But my parents don't seem to be listening. I feel as though I am living in a state of suspended animation, counting the days until I go back to my real life.

After a few days, my dad asks me if I have thought about a career. I hesitate. He mentions big corporations, stresses the satisfaction of being part of a large organisation, how you can start at the bottom and claw your way up to the top. I say nothing, but inside myself I am appalled. I have no clear ideas about what I want to do in the future and am too completely engrossed in the present. But I already know that my father's kind of life would be death to me – a life of 9 to 5 and hellish hard work. No amount of money would compensate me for it. I keep silent but I know that I want to be part of a very different world – a world of poetry, or drama. Perhaps the television? Or theatre?

But, for now, I must hold my tongue, for I have no money of my own and I rely on my father's allowance to get me through college. One day soon, I will have money of my own, and be free to live my life the way I want to live it, but for now, I have to pay lip service to his ideas. I am bored stiff here in Hertfordshire.

I slope off to my room, anxious to count the days until my return journey to Dublin. I want to avoid any conflict during this visit. I miss Kielty and Mariam and all my friends. I write to Kielty and wait for a reply. Then a scrawled letter arrives. The tone is exuberant and cheerful. Maybe written when he was in his cups. I treasure it and re-read it every day.

Chapter 9

AT LAST, I AM back in Dublin. It is the start of another academic year. Brian and I became the best of friends, but we got off to a bad start.

It was Mariam who first introduced him to the kitchen in the flat we shared on Lower Mount Street. I took a dislike to him. He was loud and cocksure and he never left any milk in the fridge for my tea.

"Oh, it's you again," I said at last one day. "Last time you came, you drank all the tea, and never even left a drop of milk in the house!" My tea was sacrosanct.

He was cheeky and unrepentant. "Oh my God, all the milk! Did I? What an animal. Jesus, I deserve to be flogged!"

He made everyone there laugh at my expense.

"You have no manners," I said then, "and no class either," just for good measure.

"Oh well," replied Brian. "We can't all be English with great manners!"

"English my arse!" I said then, quickly descending from my high horse.

"My grandparents on both sides were Irish. I'll bet I'm more Irish than you are! Brian doesn't sound very Irish to me!"

"Well, well," said Brian, holding up a hand, "Don't excite yourself, Cathleen Ni Houlihan. I'm off now anyway… I'm sick to death of all this talk of tea!"

We never would have become friends if it had not been for Karl. Karl was Brian's friend and co-creator. Small and slight and sandy-haired, he was the exact opposite to Brian: sensitive, kind, complicated, and devoid of ego. Karl was also extremely funny. This sometimes made Brian very jealous, because he wanted to be the funny man. When Sonja and I would be sweating with laughter at Karl's antics, Brian would go into a sulky rage.

There was a greater bone of contention, for both Karl and Brian wanted Sonja.

Sonja is German and exotic. She has a very chic and very expensive-looking haircut. She always wears a long gabardine, a short black skirt, dark stockings, and black court shoes. She too is studying English literature. It is not clear why she is in Dublin. She has no great interest in or feeling for the Irish or Irish culture. She is from Cologne, and she dreams of being a famous actress. She has the looks for it, the kind of bone structure that photographs so well it is a miracle. Brian has taken some wonderful black and white shots of her. She knows exactly how to look at the camera, she is not in the slightest bit self-conscious.

We are sitting in some dump of a café on Rathmines Lower, me and Brian and Sonja. Brian and Sonja are now in what is loosely termed 'a relationship'. They are not getting on. Brian is clumsily cheerful, while Sonja sits silently by. The curtain of her hair hangs over one side of her face, but it is not necessary to see her expression. She orders a coffee from the round little waitress with hauteur.

"How was Switzerland?" I venture to ask her. She smokes and begins to talk.

She spent the summer in Lausanne, with some crazy old great aunt. She was hired to be some sort of companion. Her main duties seemed to have been taking care of the old woman's silly little dogs.

She tells me how mortifying it was, sitting in restaurants and cafes and having to mop up after the ageing pooches when they wet themselves or vomited. Brian points out that it could have been worse – "you might have had to mop up after the old dame, instead!"

Sonja shoots him a disdainful glare, she is not amused. Still, we are impressed by the money she has earned. She has returned to Dublin at the start of the term with £2,000!

Brian spent the summer in Munich. It was not a success. He migrated to one of the huge campsites where so many other Irish students ended up. Everyone kept assuring him how easy it would be to obtain work, but Brian had no such luck. He put up his tent and slept in it at night. During the day, he pounded the pavements in search of a job. No one seemed to want him. He quickly ran out of money and would hang around the campsite in the evenings tortured by the smell of other people's barbecues, and wishing he had the money to go to the nearest McDonalds and stuff himself.

"What is it about the Irish" he mused. "I wandered about night after night, and everybody would keep saying, have you found yourself any work yet? No? Ah well, then, come and have a beer, but they would never offer me a bite to eat! I used to walk around, pissed out of my head because no one ever offered me a bite to eat – just bloody beer!"

Disaster finally struck when one of his tent pegs went missing in the night, and his tent collapsed. At this point, he didn't even have the money to replace a tent peg, so he went to a shop and tried to steal one. He sneaked it into his pocket and shuffled towards the exit, only to hear the teutonic screams of the sharp-eyed shop assistant, "Halt! Halt!" He fled, but alas, not quickly enough, and was caught by some keen passers-by.

He spent the night in a police cell with a bunch of wide-eyed Turkish immigrants. He was too afraid of them to sleep, and spent a sweaty night, pressed uneasily up against the cell wall, eyeing them warily. It was a mighty relief when he was let out the next day. He decided he couldn't take it anymore, so he cadged a lift off some bloke in a van, and borrowed some money to get home. He said he never wanted to see Munich again.

I envied him his adventures. Compared to my quiet time in Hertfordshire, he had had a colourful summer. There was only one thing of note to report; my father had been given a new posting. They were moving to France, to a place called Mulhouse in Alsace. It didn't sound all that exciting, but it might be a bit more interesting than Hertfordshire. I didn't intend to spend much time there anyway. My life in Dublin would open out, and with any luck, I would secure work and financial independence before the end of the next academic year. With any luck, I wouldn't need to go back to my parents for any more summers. I would be independent, and my life would be permanently in Dublin.

Chapter 10

THE DAY WEARS ON and gradually loses its magic. I have failed to attend my Shakespeare lecture yet again. I am filled with dissatisfaction with myself for not attending. My academic timetable is sparse enough, barely twelve hours of contact time per week, so it is daft not to turn up for what's on offer. Truth is, the loose timetable is sapping the energy out of me. The more time I have, the less I seem able to do. I have so much free time – what am I supposed to do with it?

The hours pass as I drift around the campus, hoping to bump into someone, looking for a diversion. I am losing all discipline, and the mere idea of sitting at a desk in the Lecky library seems impossible. I am constantly strapped for cash, and even a coffee in Bewley's is a treat that

I have to account for these days. The hours are difficult to fill.

It's February, a hateful month. Preferable to January only in the fact that it is shorter. A dull grey sky sits loweringly above my head, and a bad-tempered wind blows litter and leaves in little eddies along the pavements. The city wears a bored, grumpy look, and Trinity squats behind its centuries of unlovely dirt. It starts to rain, so I swerve into Suffolk Street and up the speckled stone steps into O'Neill's. I stumble in and throw my bag and coat on the little seat facing the door.

I listen out for Kielty's voice and sure enough, I hear him talking to a couple of lecturers. He is quieter than usual, and not showing off. When he sees me he offers me a drink, but when it comes, I am not invited to join them. So I sit in my corner, and delve into my satchel for the book of essays on Joyce that I got earlier in Hanna's Bookshop. I will show Kielty that I did not come in here solely on the lookout for him. I will show him, and myself, that I am serious about my studies and that I have a college life independent of him. All the same, I can't help wishing his cronies would go away so I could have him to myself.

Chapter 11

PADDY AND SUZANNE ARE warning me off Kielty. "He's terrible, Anna, why do you hang around with him?" They tell me that he is a brute. He has traumatised Suzanne by ripping her t-shirt with his bare teeth. The awful deed took place one afternoon last week when a group of them went into O'Neill's and had the misfortune to attract Kielty's attention when they were ordering their drinks. Alerted by their Northern accents, Kielty began to banter with them but when they did not appreciate his wit he turned nasty and that was when he leant forward and tore Suzanne's t-shirt.

This is the sort of unfortunate incident that gives Kielty his bad reputation. On a par with the time he got talking to my beautiful friend Sarah and cheekily asked her ".. and what colour are your knickers?" On one level I am convinced that he engineers these little scenes – they are part and parcel of what is expected of him as a drunken, outrageous poet.

****

It is a summer's evening, I wander around Front Square at a loose end. I don't feel like going back to the flat and I don't feel like seeking out any friends. The womb of Trinity seems to hold me in its quiet peace, and I don't want to leave its precinct.

Out of the corner of my eye, I catch sight of someone jacketed slipping into Players Theatre. Must be a rehearsal on? I nip over to spy, but the door to the little theatre is already shut. No way of watching without being seen. I lean against the grey bricks of beloved Trinity and drink in the air. It is an unusually beautiful evening. Dusk has descended late and birdsong still echoes in the quad. The air is soft and lilac-coloured, and almost tangible. I am twenty years old and I do not yet know that an evening such as this is a unique blessing, something precious that must not be taken for granted. This is the time of my life. My heart is full; full of the love of life, and longing, and dreams. I long to see Kielty.

Across the devilish cobblestones, past the Campanile, and into New Square, a slight change in atmosphere in this newer part of the college.

My Faithful Heart

Into number 32 and up the stairs. My heart is beating quite fast now. I stand before his door and listen for him. Not easy to tell if Kielty is in or not, for unlike other people he does not need the hum of radio or the rumble of the TV for company. All such things he regards as a distraction, a waste of time. Some well-meaning woman had once brought him a radio because she was surprised he didn't have one. But Kielty quickly got rid of it. 'Nothing but silly noise' was his verdict.

Women from all over Ireland visited him after hearing his mellow Kerry accents at poetry readings, or on the radio. All kinds of women. Sometimes they behaved with decorum, and sometimes they didn't. He told me about them once, in awe of them, in amusement. He did not mock them, but he made no secret of his puzzlement. He was amazed by women's hearts, and the desires housed in the most unlikely bodies. Some of them came bearing strange gifts – the radio was one – but another woman brought him a present of a fish, a big fresh salmon. She presented him with it, and then she lay down on the carpet and commanded him to make love to her. He said it was a terrible thing that women think poets always want to have loads of sex all over the place, and it was a hard thing to live up to.

My thoughts were running round my head.... What if he had some woman in there with him now, I would be mortified. But still, I knocked. A moment's silence and then I heard him shuffle to the door. He opened it and shook his grizzly head at me grumpily.

"Come in," he said, then frowning. "What is it you want?"

I didn't know what to reply. I looked at him. He was strangely attired in a one-piece body-suit thing – long johns, I suppose. I'd never seen anyone in them before.

"What on earth are you wearing?" I said.

"Ah, I have to get trussed up tonight," he said, "I've to go and read at Dublin Castle." He didn't look as though he expected to enjoy himself. For once, I had the advantage. I began to smile in amusement.

"Don't stand there laughing at me, make yourself useful." He fished in his desk drawer and retrieved a bank note. "Take this over to Jimmy, and fetch me a naggin of Jameson's, will you?"

Would I? Of course, I would. I would have done anything for him, though I tried to hide it.

I took the note from his fingers and left. I felt happy to be walking over the cobbles again, on my errand of mercy. I had been chosen for something. Out of Front Gate and along the well-worn path to Suffolk Street I trudged, pushing open the door and entering into the warmth of the gabbling, jostling throng in O'Neill's. I got to the bar and waited for Jimmy, head barman, to notice me. He served with speed and authority, like a priest in his formal black trousers and clean white shirt. In all my time in O'Neill's, I had never seen Jimmy have a drink. A tall, well-built man in his forties, with a mass of greying curls, Jimmy saw a lot and knew everyone's secrets. But like a priest in the confessional, he was silent as the grave, a total professional.

As I ordered the naggin, his knowing eyes rested on mine for a moment. He would know it was for Kielty. Was there disapproval in his eyes as he took the note from me? I did not wait to see, but hurried back to New Square, to Kielty.

By now Kielty was fully attired in his unwonted evening dress of black tails, white shirt etc. It was quite a transformation, but although he looked smart, it didn't suit him. He looked swollen and uncomfortable out of his usual clothes. His face was pink and scrubbed, his medium length, thin wavy hair stuck down on his skull. His short fat torso strained at the seams of his formal suit. He caught my gaze and glanced away, embarrassed. "Give me that," he said hurriedly, swiping the solid little bottle in its brown paper bag from me.

I left soon after that, for his mood was sombre. I thought it was a bit of a sell-out, to be honest, him going to read his poems in Dublin Castle. I don't think his Kerry ancestors would have been very impressed. Still, we all have to make a living.

I walked slowly back to the flat in Lower Mount Street where Mariam was curled up in front of the telly. "Look at this!" she exclaimed as I entered. "It's only Kielty on the news!"

I said nothing, only watched as he performed, saying the words to a rapt audience. Kielty was like a Rubik's cube – multi-faceted, complex. A complete puzzle.

Chapter 12

THERE ARE DAYS LIKE this when the hours hang heavy on my hands. No money, too much time. My literature courses seem ponderous, self-indulgent, and esoteric. I want to be part of the city life I see around me – smartly dressed people rush importantly to and from jobs, and in the evenings they have money to go to bars and restaurants.

I have outgrown my studies, but there isn't any way forward. My body is at its peak, throbbing with life, finely tuned to every heartbeat and murmur. Although I still love novels and poetry unconditionally, I find it difficult to sit for many hours in the Lecky library, adding my sighs and squirms of impatience to the tense atmosphere. And I wish I had money for pretty new clothes.

Coming out of Grafton Street I bump into Kielty. I eye him warily, sizing up his mood. He has been drinking, and he is full of mischief. His face is flushed and his eyes are bright. He hails me with enthusiasm.

"Just look at you!" he beams at me. "You're like a queen – a queen lost and erring in a democratic world!" I blush at the compliment. I'm very flattered. He makes me feel wonderful when he is like this, smiling at me and giving me all his attention.

"I've had a lovely day," he tells me. "I spent it drinking with two beautiful women from Brussels. One of them is amazing, Adele. Do you know her?"

I reply sulkily in the affirmative. I've seen her hanging round the Arts Block. She's a mature student, and her father is a diplomat. It is clear she only attends Trinity for something to fill the hours. She drifts around in a fur coat, drinking coffee and chattering endlessly. She is attractive and sophisticated and monied. I am jealous of Kielty's admiration for her, and I am in no mood to humour him.

"Yeah, I know her," I say unenthusiastically. Then for good measure: "Actually, I can't stand her."

Kielty looks amazed.

"Why? What has she done to you?"

He tells me I need a drink, and I follow him into The Berni Inn where he orders us drinks; a whiskey for him and a glass of Guinness for me. Then he continues to sing Adele's praises. It is really getting on my nerves now.

"I hate her." I announce suddenly.

Kielty looks astonished. "Why?"

A hundred reasons rush to my mind. I hate her because she has poise. She seems to have loads of money, she wears a fur coat and she doesn't care. I hate her because Kielty has spent the day with her and because he won't stop singing her praises. I try to put it into words. In the end, all I come out with is:

"She doesn't care a damn about poets or poetry," I say.

"I dunno, she seems to like poetry well enough," says Kielty. "Anyway she's good company. I enjoyed myself." He is unusually self-satisfied and pleased with himself. I want to puncture his smugness. I take a gulp of my drink, and then I say spitefully,

"You know Kielty, here in Dublin you're famous and all that, and everyone thinks you're the bee's knees, but I can tell you that in England nobody has even heard of you!"

But he only chuckles at me. "Of course they have!"

"Honestly, they haven't. You're only a big fish in a small pond."

He looks a bit annoyed at this, but he only laughs. "Well, Burdey," he says. "You've a great line in insult!"

I'm sorry now, I wish I hadn't said it. I can't breathe and my throat aches. But I won't give in. He downs another gulp of whiskey, saying, "I must go now"

So first I was his queen, and now I bore him.

He gets up and leaves the pub quickly, on his way back to the Arts Block. Probably time for another lecture, or seminar. His lectures are very popular, the hall is always full. The amazing thing about Kielty is he never misses a lecture or appointment or is even late. He has amazing stamina and unlike me, he is totally committed to what he is doing. His teaching never bores him, and he is always passionate about literature.

****

Lately, my love for Kielty had become tainted with resentment. I couldn't stand it when he talked other people up in front of me. Did he do it on purpose or what? Fancy telling me how much he liked that silly Adele. In the beginning, he had been very complimentary to me, asking me questions about my background and telling me I was very bright. But nowadays he made me feel like I had slipped down the ladder of his esteem somehow. I began to compose bitter little poems about him, obliquely accusing him of misogyny and meanness. I was in my Sylvia Plath phase then, so I had a good role model. I remember I wrote one poem that I was particularly pleased with, and shoved it under the door to his rooms.

There! I thought to myself. That should shake him!

I pictured his face as he read it, how shocked he would be. I couldn't wait to hear what he would say. Maybe he would apologise to me, say he was sorry for hurting my feelings.

I had to wait a day or two, but eventually I fell into step next to him as he walked past the Campanile one morning. He greeted me affably and we walked on together. I stole a sideways look at him and saw that he was in one of his morose moods. Maybe it was because my poem had been too close to the mark? I was more than willing to forgive him, I just wanted him to show a bit of humility. But he said nothing about any poem. Impatiently, I said "Well, did you get it? My poem?"

"Oh yes, the poem. Yes, I got your poem."

"Well?" I said.

"Oh, very Plathian," he said drily, "very Plathian indeed."

I was very annoyed. He didn't even seem bothered. Totally maddening. I strode away quickly then, in a huff. We often disagreed about things. I loved hearing his lectures, but that didn't mean I shared a lot of his opinions. And I was pretty sure my poem was a good effort.

Chapter 13

I DECIDED I HAD better try and date a man my own age. I met John O'Driscoll in the Buttery one evening, and we got on well. He was attractive in a very fresh, pure way, with pale freckled skin, and lots of black curly hair. He was taller than me and he spoke with a breathy West of Ireland accent which I liked.

Over the next fortnight, we got to know each other a bit. We made appointments to meet in bars, and I spent a long time getting ready for each one. As we sat in bars, we spoke about ourselves. I had not got much to say, my family life seemed too dull to talk about, and my sole love interest was Kielty, and I couldn't tell John about that. We ended up talking about his love life — at least he had one. By the sound of it he was still in love with her, some young girl from back home. It had all the hallmarks of a fairy tale.

He was a poor lad from the town, she was the only daughter of a wealthy farmer who had stacks of land. They used to meet in secret, and make love in a little barn on her father's land that she had customised for the purpose. They would spend secret afternoons together, larking about in the summer fields, and then in the barn. John's eyes took on a faraway look as he rhapsodised about her. "She always brought me an apple," he said softly.

"An apple?" I echoed stupidly, thinking the whole thing was beginning to sound unbelievably biblical. "What for?"

"Because after we had finished making love I was always really hungry." I thought this was very innocent and sweet, but it kind of took the edge off the romance, imagining him crunching away on his apple as his girlfriend put her clothes back on.

It all ended badly for John. His girlfriend's father got wise to their antics and stormed into the barn one fateful afternoon. John described him as a mighty hulk of a man, over six foot tall, with broad muscular shoulders, and shaking a massive stick. He chased John off his property and warned him that if he ever came near his daughter again he would rip his balls off. John was a gentle soul and took the threat very seriously. He never saw his girlfriend again. Yet another life blighted by a domineering father. Although I was sympathetic, I wished that John would seem a bit less in love with his ex-girlfriend, and a bit more in love with me. I was growing bored and jealous of his references to her. In vain I tried to steer the conversation away from his Eden-like love trysts. No good. One evening we decide to call it a day and we didn't meet up anymore.

Then I dated another bloke. He was studying dentistry, which he hated. He explained that he had to study it because his father had said he wouldn't pay for him to do anything useful, like the arts. He was afraid of his father, although I don't think he had ever been hit by him. Like me, he couldn't wait to finish his degree and get his own income and independence. With a degree in dentistry, he stood a better chance than me.

He had nice hair – pale red-gold, and wavy. But the trouble was after we spent bouts of passionate kissing, his stubble had rubbed my chin practically red raw. Sometimes this meant I had to stay in for a day or two until it healed. But once, not wanting to miss a lecture, I covered it up with talcum powder and foundation and braved it. I entered Front Gate and saw Kielty coming towards me. He was chatting to some girl, and as he approached he glanced my way. I felt anxious, as I knew my poorly disguised raw chin would not escape his eagle eye. I was right. As I veered away from him, he grabbed me by the arm. He peered into my face, saying to his companion "Did you ever see anything like the state of this chin? My God."

Then he said to me, "Who have you been eating the face off?! You've nearly rubbed your chin away! What a sight!" He turned away from me with a look of disgust. The girl he was with gave me a sympathetic glance, as I bolted off, red with embarrassment. I told myself he had reacted like that because he was jealous, but I knew it was no such thing. He despised me, and it cut me to the quick. There was no point in going with these young men, looking for love. I didn't care a damn about them.

Chapter 14

THERE WAS ONE OTHER candidate. We started out as friends. He was older than me, short and stocky and sandy-haired. He was doing an MA on Yeats and he was Irish/American. We got talking one day in the Arts Block when he knocked over his polystyrene cup of coffee, and I helped him mop up. His name was James McNulty and his family left Belfast because of the troubles when he was a boy and went to America. We had something in common. Like me, he loved Yeats and had come back to Ireland to reconnect with his roots. He talked to me intelligently

"The more I read Yeats, the more I wonder," he mused. "Does anyone really know what he means?"

I got impatient. "It's not a question of knowing what he means, it's that he sounds absolutely right! It feels totally right!" I said. "Why must you murder everything with analysis?"

I told him that I was fed up with thinking all the time and fed up with being an undergraduate. He looked at me shrewdly and said:

"Are you sure you're bored? Or could it just be that you can't concentrate?" I blushed and looked away. How could I explain?

I just wanted my life to begin.

We went to McDaid's and I sat back in a warm corner of the bar while he got us drinks. I looked around without much interest. It was Friday night and the place was full. The swell of voices round me rose and fell, but I was strangely cut off from the scene. I felt sad but at peace. I knew I wouldn't bump into Kielty in McDaid's. James came and sat next to me. He put our drinks down in front of us and shoved his satchel with all his books and papers carefully under the seats. I'd seen his work. His writing was very neat and precise, and he annotated everything in a very scholarly way. But tonight I didn't want to talk about poetry. I confided in James about Kielty. He nodded wisely. He said that Kielty was a mixed-up, unhappy man, not over his failed marriage. He said I should steer clear.

"How about sex?" he asked suddenly.

I didn't know what to answer. I dreaded him finding out I still hadn't done it properly. But I think he had guessed. He confided that sex was not easy to get in Dublin. He could do with some.

"What's it really like to go all the way?" I asked him. He thought for a moment and then said.

"It's great, really great."

I wanted to talk to him but somehow I just couldn't relax. I felt that he was thinking of me in terms of assuaging his hunger. For some reason, the idea filled me with dread.

When we left the pub, he tried to kiss me, But his nose banged into my cheek and I stepped back from him. "Have I scared you off?" he asked softly. I turned away and marched off, pretending not to have heard.

The next evening, I went to a party in a big house in Rathgar. It was full of bright young things from the Southside, dressed in the latest Pia Bang fashions, and insipid young men in ties, who were reading law. I felt out of it. I thought I should have persevered with James but I had the feeling I had blown that. I wondered how it was possible to feel even lonelier in crowds like this, but it was certainly true.

I downed several glasses of wine, but when I'm sad alcohol has little effect on me, and so I wandered glumly around from room to room making occasional attempts to join in conversations.

Everyone seemed to be in the middle of a hilarious story or joke, but I could never follow it properly, having missed the vital beginning.

I wandered into the kitchen and helped myself to some canapés. There was a friendly cat who cheered me up by jumping up on my knee and purring as if it liked me. I felt sure no one else did.

I finally got a lift home from some of the aforementioned bright young things, who were heading back to Killiney. I could think of nothing to say as I sat in the car, my chest felt tight and aching, and when at last they dropped me off I heard myself thank them in a thin, colourless voice I hardly recognised as my own.

When I got in, the flat was empty. So I went straight to my room and climbed into bed. I lay there thinking about everything. About how desperate I had been to come back to Ireland, how important it was to me. But none of the young people at the party seemed interested in Irish politics past or present. The Easter Rising was never mentioned. None of the things that resonated with me were ever mentioned in

Trinity circles – not Bloody Sunday, or Michael Collins or Bobby Sands and the hunger strikers.

I felt isolated, as though my brand of Irishness were out of date, redundant. I fell into an uneasy sleep and when I woke up, I found myself thinking about Patrick Pearse. I had been reading up about him, and some of the details haunted me. I thought of how they had come for him in the early hours of the morning, for he was executed at 3am. I lay in the dark and wondered if he had been able to sleep beforehand, or had he lain there, too afraid to sleep, with his heart pounding with fear. Even with his courage and sense of conviction, he must have felt terrible fear when he was blindfolded, as he heard the armed men before him take their orders, taking up position to send their bullets into his body.

And what about them – his executors, what about them? The doomed chosen ones, picked out at random to perform this awful duty? Did they know anything about the young man they were to kill? Did they realise that he was an idealist, a poet, and a teacher? Did they flinch as they aimed? And did they feel sick when he crumpled to the ground?

Who cared about any of this now? Nobody at Trinity. Maybe I should have gone to Belfield. But the campus just wasn't beautiful like Trinity was.

Patricia Burgess-McCormick

Romantic Ireland's dead and gone,

It's with O'Leary in the grave...

(W.B. Yeats)

I lay there feeling sorry for myself until at last I fell back asleep.

Chapter 15

BRIAN, SONJA AND I are at a loose end. Brian, never short of ideas, makes a suggestion.

"I know," he says brightly. "Let's go round to my place and have a séance. Karl might be there, with four of us, it could be really good."

We agree to go. I am curious as I haven't ever done a séance, and Sonja is hoping to see Karl. We follow Brian through flat little dusty streets to his digs in a tiny little terraced house. As he turns the lock in the front door, there is the sound of little footsteps scampering to meet us in a hurry. Barely have we entered the hallway when a wizened little woman, with grey hair in a bun, accosts Brian.

"Now, Mr Barry," she says accusingly in a high-pitched, scratchy voice. "You have not yet paid me this week's rent."

Brian moves determinedly towards the staircase, full of confidence.

"Don't you worry about that, now, Mrs Nugent, that will all be taken care of in the very near future." As he tries to sweep us past her, she fixes her bright little beady eyes on me and Sonja.

"I do not like to see you bringing young women up to your rooms." She says. "This is a respectable house and I know what you young Trinity students are like." But Brian will have no more of her. Firmly he puts a hand on my back and Sonja's and pushes us up the staircase in front of him.

"Mrs Nugent, I am hurt that you should think badly of these two very respectable friends of mine. Sonja here is all the way from Germany, and Anna here is from England!"

"England!" echoes the little woman, as if he had said 'Gomorrah'. She continues to hector him as we reach the top of the stairs but Brian is no longer paying her any attention. He is trying to put the key in the lock to his bedsit. This is difficult as there is no light, neither natural nor electric, and a fusty smell is everywhere. At last, he pushes the door open and we are inside.

What a strange little flat it is. Karl appears and gives us a guided tour. It lasts all of 5 minutes. There are two tiny bedrooms and a tiny living room. There are no windows anywhere. The whole living space has been carved out of an airless attic.

The four of us assemble enough chairs and sit round the rickety little table. We call up random spirits until Karl baulks at the atmosphere. He gets up suddenly from the table and walks out of the room. The spell is broken. Brian is annoyed. Sonja and I go after Karl to see if he is okay.

"He's not like you, Brian, He's sensitive," says Sonja. I am inclined to agree. Anyway, the séance was giving me the creeps.

Chapter 16

IT'S A WET SATURDAY and I have no money. At least Mariam had no plans to go out either. She rose late and sat around in her slippers and glasses reading a book on Ella Fitzgerald and curling her frizzy hair between her thumb and forefinger, a habit which I find curiously soothing to watch. I put on a Billie Holliday cassette and drink endless cups of tea. "My man don't love me, he treats me awful mean..." God, I felt blue. I persuade her to put on some Grace Jones instead: "Pull up to the bumper, baby!"

The drops of rain pattered endlessly.

"What are you thinking about?" asked Mariam.

I was standing leaning by the window, holding back the curtains so I could see outside.

I was silent for a bit. Then I turned and said: "This is no country for young women......"

I read a bit of Yeats, but his beautiful love poems only made me sadder when I remembered they had been inspired by a love that was unrequited. I remembered Kielty's words; "poetry is the only thing that matters". Was it true? Did the feelings not matter then, only the poetry? To me, they were one and the same thing. I rejected the academic take on it. Surely the poems were only important to people because of the feelings they spoke about – feelings that people recognised and identified with.

Mariam's laboratory rat rumbled gloomily around his wheel in his cage in the corner of the sitting room. He annoyed me vaguely with his flittery, scrabbling little movements. When would he realise he wasn't going anywhere on that wheel?

Now that Mariam had given up her MA studies on adipose tissue, he had an uncertain future. I asked her what she intended to do with him. She looked up from Ella with a thoughtful expression.

"I suppose I should let him go." I agreed. It was hardly fair to subject the unfortunate morsel to another postgraduate's experimentation on his adipose tissue.

We decided that we would release the lab-bred brute into the open. So later on we dressed in scarves and hats and carried him, cage and all, up to Stephens Green. A Garda looked at us suspiciously, but eventually, we let the rat go near the Markievizc statue. He scuttled off stupidly and disappeared among the soggy winter leaves.

"Wonder how long he'll last," sighed Mariam.

I looked up at the lowering grey skies and thought an hour seemed a reasonable guess, but I said nothing because I knew she already felt guilty about him. Her failure to make any sense of a PhD also meant that she had to find another excuse if she wanted to stay on in Ireland. She could only legally stay if she were a student but her parents were putting a lot of pressure on her to return to Africa. They never intended her to stay beyond her primary degree. They didn't seem to grasp that Mariam, having spent more than two-thirds of her life in Ireland, felt very attached to it.

We walked back down Grafton Street and treated ourselves to two cheese croissants from the French stall. That left us with very little money so we headed back to the flat with a carton of milk for more tea and toast.

When we got back to the flat, Paddy and Kevin had come in. This was good news as

Paddy, being from Northern Ireland, and so having a British student grant, was always flush. I borrowed a few bob off her to buy some Polish coal. We wanted to build a nice fire and stay in and watch a Bette Davis film that was on late that night.

The newsagent where we bought our emergencies was in Pearse Street. They always stared at us because we weren't locals. They especially stared at Mariam because she was black and rich looking. I bought a copy of 'An Phoblacht' just so they'd accept us a bit more. I enjoyed looking at it and trying to make sense of the headlines. But I'd forgotten most of the Irish I had learned at primary school in County Tyrone and I might as well have been trying to read Greek.

Then back to the flat...What am I doing with myself?

Chapter 17

THE MARKS FOR OUR end of year assignments are out. This mark matters as it will go towards our final degree grade. A group of students press excitedly around the board where the page is pinned. I feel confident that I will have a decent mark. As the heads before me clear and I am able to find my name on the list, my heart jolts with shock and then sinks.

My mark is much lower than I was expecting. This is humiliating. I turn away and make my way down the Arts Block stairs. I knew it was a mistake to have done the American literature course but Kielty had warned me off doing the Yeats one. He said he couldn't have me in his seminar. It wouldn't work. In vain I had remonstrated that I loved Yeats but he shook his shaggy head. "Sorry, Burdey. It can't happen."

Looking back, I hadn't argued very hard. For sure, it would have been awkward, but now my mark was living proof that I didn't understand American literature or lectures.

I felt tears pricking my eyes and stopped to locate a hanky. Blindly, I hurried across Front Square towards O'Neill's. I needed to see Kielty. He would help me. Up the speckled steps and through the door, past the mirror with the familiar Red Hand on it. Sure enough, there he stood at the bar, with two of his cronies, enjoying a pint. He caught sight of me and nodded warily. "I need a word with you," I said.

"What? Can't you see I'm busy now?"

But I insisted. He left his pint on the bar and followed me around the corner where we could be private. I blurted out about my marks, and he shrugged.

"It's nothing to do with me!" he protested.

"But it is!" I argued, "you wouldn't let me do the Yeats!"

He shook his head, his plump white fingers spread in denial. He wouldn't admit anything. Fury rose in me, unstoppable.

"It's because of you!" I blurted out.

"Burdey," he was murmuring and touching me on the arm. There was a hint of pity in his voice.

How dare he. I thought of all these months, all my hopeful love, and how he had twisted it into some sorry, sick thing. I raised my hand and slapped his face. As soon as I had done it, I felt a terrible regret mixed with fear and a kind of elation. He stumbled slightly, stepping back from me, and stood, mouth slightly open. He seemed to sway, hand to his cheek. Now I was babbling breathlessly;

"You messed me around. You never cared about me. Never! You were just playing with me!"

I saw the confusion and shock on his face. I wanted to cry, to throw my arms around him, to hug him, but my rage was uppermost and the shock in his face told me it would be useless, so useless. I was suffocating as we stood, looking at each other, both somehow frozen. Then the door to the snug creaked open and his crony's voice broke the stalemate. "Kielty? Are you alright?"

He ignored me completely. Of course, for I was of no account in their world of male camaraderie and drinks and jokes. I was nothing. Kielty shuffled backwards, away from me, and moved back to the bar. Casey shot me a brief, hostile glance, before turning away and following Kielty back to the bar where their pints stood waiting for them. They would soon forget all about me.

PART 2

Chapter 18

Love is a stranger

In an open car

To tempt you in

And drive you far away......

(Eurythmics - Love is a Stranger)

MY PRAYERS WERE ANSWERED. My saviour came and he was from the land of love, from Italy. He wore glamour like a magic mantle. His eyes were dark and full of promise. He was mysterious and funny. With his largesse he blew the last barrier out of my mind, he saved me from myself, our affair was a blessed escape. He introduced me to sex and love, with honesty.

The day we met was the first in a fortnight of glorious sunshine which is not usual in Ireland.

In a newsagent in Lower Mount Street, the shopkeeper was warning us all.

"I'm telling you now, it's not natural this sunshine. Watch out, it goes to people's heads, makes them do strange things!"

I laughed. It was the first time I had really laughed in a while. I was beginning to feel better. The pain was still there when I thought about Kielty, but I was able to forget it sometimes. Shortly after this, I met him – my Deliverer.

I was in the National Gallery in Merrion Square, looking at paintings. I wandered from space to space, soothing my heart by giving myself something different to look at. A handsome foreign gentleman joined me politely. Then he caught my eye and smiled at me. He nodded at the painting in front of us and said, "No fun to be an artist, eh? They don't love you until you are dead. Then they make loads of money from your work!" He chuckled.

I couldn't help laughing. This was certainly a new way of looking at things. We went and had a coffee in the adjacent café, and he introduced himself. His name was Claudio and he was from Italy. He was just here on business, working as a rep for Fiat.

He was very keen to take me out, but although I found him entertaining I felt uneasy with him and declined. We parted but not before he had persuaded me to give him my phone number.

He rang and rang for over a week. Then one evening, I was alone in the flat and he rang and asked me for a date. I gave in and agreed to let him take me out for dinner. It turned out to be a fateful decision.

For ten days we explored the Dublin coast together in the sunshine and his Alfa Romeo. It was a beautiful car. It was shiny and navy and it had white leather seats. The number plate said 'ROMA' in stylish orange letters, and when we drove through Bray, children who were playing in the street, or their gardens waved and shouted, "Roma! Roma!" at us in excitement. I felt like a film star.

We drove in the sunshine to the Powerscourt Gardens and dined in a glass restaurant suspended over a sparkling river. We drove to Dalkey and feasted on lobster in a deliciously intimate restaurant where the white linen tablecloths shone under candlelight. It was clear that Claudio was very taken with me. I thought I had never been so happy.

We sped through the Dublin mountains. Time did not exist. Only the sun and the glorious scenery. At lunchtime, we stopped at a beautiful restaurant. We ordered lobster and Orvieto. Smart waiters served us lavish desserts from golden trolleys. We ate strawberries with Maraschino. Another favourite was fruit salad with Cointreau. The beauty of life when laced with good food and drink and warm sunshine became a daily miracle with Claudio in my life.

I thought it would be perfect to live like this for a while, He seemed to have unlimited cash. Then one day he told me he had spent everything.

"Yes. In the last week I have spent all my savings. Now I will have to go to work again."

Oh dear. So the party was over. Still, I looked at his craggy, tanned face. His dark, canny eyes were not worried. They danced. There would be more good times.

"Six thousand pounds, I have spent ….we had a good time, eh?" He laughed softly and reached for my hand across the immaculate Irish linen table cloth.

I looked out of the window we were seated by. It was dusk, on a perfect June evening. Dublin bay glistened before us, placid and beautiful. Lights were just beginning to twinkle around her edges. I knew I never wanted to live anywhere else.

Over the last few days, my brain had had plenty of time to rest. Now it began to heave into action.

"Where will you go to make money?" I asked gently.

"Oh, I will have to go abroad. It's not so easy to do much business here in Ireland, but I will come back in a few months. I will get a flat for us here, yes? You can wait for me."

Perfect. My heart soared. I could have my freedom, see my friends, get on with my acting and writing. Maybe generate some income with my short stories and poems. It was a dream come true, a perfect existence. I turned and smiled at him. All my hope and joy was in my smile.

"Yes," I said,

"Yes, that sounds lovely."

Chapter 19

AT THE END OF that Trinity term, I packed my belongings and headed off to Dublin airport. I felt the usual dread even though I had a new and powerful ally in Claudio. He would make it possible for me to stay in Dublin with or without my father's support. My parents had recently moved from Hertfordshire in England to France, and so I was not returning to Hertfordshire. I was weary of all the moving for my dad's job, but most of all I was worried because France was even further away from Dublin. There wasn't even an airport in Mulhouse, the nearest one was in Basel, which was in neighbouring Switzerland.

I disembarked from the plane at Basel and met my parents with a sense of triumph. I felt that I was a woman now, and soon I would be beyond their control. My mother seemed pleased with the change in me. When we got back to the house she took me aside and asked, "Have you met someone?"

I nodded. She was pleased and wanted to know more. I answered with caution and reserve, knowing that a foreign 39-year-old was not going to seem like good news to my parents. Nor was I certain of my feelings for him. The last few weeks had been a kind of whirlwind.

Mulhouse was the town in Alsace where my family was now entombed. My father was working in a big textile company there. I was fed up with yet another foreign posting. We didn't know a soul in Alsace, and I wasn't interested in the place. I resented having to leave Dublin every break and envied with all my heart those students I knew who just went back to established family homes in other parts of Dublin or Ireland. I didn't know how I would fill in the long weeks until the start of another term.

However, I was soon caught up in a frightening drama of my own which only heightened my sense of uprootedness and alienation.

Chapter 20

IT IS THE OLDEST story in the world; my period did not come. For a few days, I hid myself away and sweated. I still hoped that it meant nothing, that my period was just late, nothing more. I lived in dread. I could concentrate on nothing. News of foreign massacres did not touch me when I watched television. The sense of dread growing in the pit of my stomach seemed more terrible. At night I went to sleep praying that I would wake to blood-stained sheets. I desperately wanted a reprieve. In the morning the sight of the unsullied bedlinen made me desperate.

I was in France, a foreign country, and though I knew the language I did not know its systems and had no doctor. I went to an information centre and was told I needed to go to the Centre

Sociale. There I did a pregnancy test. There was another girl alongside me. We were both handed plastic tubes and told to wee in them. I followed the other girl into the toilets. She walked leisurely, unconcerned. Perhaps she was married. I wished I were her. I wished I were anyone else but me. When I handed over my urine sample I stared at it. It held the secret of my future.

****

A few days later I returned. I was pregnant. Two social workers informed me of the fact. One of them was hard-faced, accusing. She asked me why I was so shocked.

She asked, "what method of contraception were you using?" I told her Coitus Interruptus. Claudio had assured me that all Italians used it. Her voice then took on a vehement note.

"But surely you must know that this is a thoroughly unreliable method? Everyone knows that!" She urged me to think about what I was going to do.

"The situation is an urgent one," she told me, as if I needed telling. My head was spinning. "You aren't married, but are you in a stable relationship? Can you rely on the father of the baby to help you? It is a tremendous financial burden and you are, after all, only a student. You must think of these things."

Her voice was an unwelcome commentary disturbing my own thoughts. I wanted her to be quiet. I felt very sick. I did not silence her as I knew I deserved to be rebuked.

Over her desk was a large poster of a pink, smiling baby. I tried to remind myself that this was the penalty for my irresponsible acts, nothing worse than a baby.

The social worker informed me of abortion as an option. "But you will have to decide quickly, the limit is 10 weeks here in France. 10 weeks, Mademoiselle, and there is a waiting list...so there is no time to waste....remember after 10 weeks no French doctor will want to touch you."

Her words heightened my nausea. Abortion was, to my ears, one of the ugliest words in the world – rating alongside 'genocide' and 'rape'. Grisly images of tiny crushed limbs and ragged foetuses grappled with each other in my head. I had heard how it was done. They would stick a hoover up me and suck it out bit by bit. At my Catholic prep school they had not sanitised its realities.

"Avorter...." Without realising it, I had murmured the word to myself. The social worker took this as assent. "Cela coutera a peu pres deux mille francs," she informed me. Deux mille francs....that was £200.

I repeated this information as well, mindlessly. She seemed to think the cost shocked me. "You mustn't let the cost put you off, after all, it will cost a lot more to bring a child into the world. Have you a choice? If you have no one to help you, you can't survive alone. You are a student with no income. Don't expect the state to shoulder the burden."

At this point I fainted. When I came round there were two women holding me up. The social worker now had a younger woman at her side. They were now very concerned. The older woman became animated. She asked me why I had fainted. "Est-ce que c'est l'emotion d'avoir un enfant?"

I muttered something about nausea. She nodded. The younger woman was very kind. She asked me where I lived.

I will drive you home," she said. "You look pale."

I was very grateful.

During the drive home I was very quiet, but she asked me a little bit about myself. I told her I was at university in Dublin, and was only in France for the holiday because my father had been relocated here for his work. I got her to stop the car some way off from the house, as I didn't want anyone in my family to see me getting out of the car, and asking lots of questions. She understood. As I climbed out of the car she leant forward and smiled at me.

"Au revoir," she said, adding, "Bon Courage, Mademoiselle!"

The next day I went to a clinic to have a scan done. 'Echographie' is the French word. A cheerful doctor led me into a little room with a television screen on a desk. I had to undress and he put a substance like Vaseline all over my tummy and then pressed a microphone thing against it which was joined to the television by a flex. It took him a while to locate the signs of life. He muttered to himself as he waved the microphone over my abdomen, then exclaimed triumphantly, "Ca y est!" I looked at the screen in front of me but I don't remember seeing anything. He gave me a print of the scan. He said the foetus was about two centimetres long. I wanted to know how formed it was. It seemed to be a bit like a comma, all head.

"Mais ça va vite, très vite!" he enthused. "In a few weeks it will have legs and arms!"

I left the clinic clutching the printout of the scan.

****

That evening I wrote to Claudio. It was a short letter and probably sounded desperate. I was not sure what his reaction would be. Very soon he rang me. He was not a man of many words. "I got your letter, Anna," he said, "I come to get you, yes?"

I almost cried with relief. I packed a few clothes and books and waited for him to fetch me and take me to Italy. I told my mother he wanted me to meet his family.

Chapter 21

HE ARRIVED A FEW days later in his navy Alfa Romeo and stayed in a nearby hotel for a night. He came and met my mother but his attentions were perfunctory. My father was away on business. That afternoon we left Alsace and travelled southwards, through the dull little towns of Northern France, and down through Zurich, Switzerland, and the well-ordered heart of central Europe.

I was still pregnant, but with Claudio by my side, my panic subsided. He didn't want me to have an abortion. I felt safe and loved. He played his Italian cassettes and sang lustily and tunelessly along to the lyrics. He made me laugh. Nothing seemed too serious. The Swiss countryside was too perfect to be real – the grass too smooth, the buildings neatly set into the picture-postcard scenery. By evening we had crossed the border into Northern Italy but people were still speaking as though they were Swiss. I realised then how porous borders are and noted with interest that even here there were massive identity problems.

Claudio, however, was ebullient and cheerful. Stopping off in little bars and cafes along the journey, he chatted to waiters and bar staff as he quaffed his tar-like little espressos. There was something unique about our journey together – new worlds seemed to spin towards me, his hands on the steering wheel guided me onwards into an unknown future, a country I had never seen before.

We drove through La Spezia in the dusk of full July, a balmy summer evening. I remember glamorous teenage couples rushed by on Vespas – the tanned legs, butterfly skirts, and wind-tossed hair of the young girls. Their confidence and beauty baffled me. I was seduced by these vital, self-assured people. Where are they now, I wonder?

Oh Love, where did you go to?

It was a long journey to Rome, and then on to the little town near Latina where he was from. I was exhausted when we arrived. It was late evening and I remember climbing out of the car and smelling the warm scented air. One of

Claudio's friends had seen us drive into the village and he followed us on his motorbike, waving and hooting his horn frantically. Claudio was laughing for joy.

"Anna! He is one of my oldest friends – we went to school together – he is called 'Il Principe' and you are 'La Principessa'."

He leant over and kissed me hard on the mouth. After the long hot car journey, he smelt of sweat and Armani. I didn't mind. I looked down the slope to the house, and a small, thin woman came out. She was in her early thirties, her wavy dark hair was not in any style, but pulled back into a ponytail. She wore a flowery housecoat and had dark shadows under her eyes.

She smiled at me and greeted Claudio. I could not understand what they were saying. They were speaking in a dialect, and no matter how hard I concentrated, the sounds they made bore little resemblance to the text book Italian I had been teaching myself.

All day we had driven on shining motorways under the intense sun, and when dusk had come, it was a relief. Now the cool night air enfolded us as Claudio and Amalia gabbled excitedly at each other, and were joined by Claudio's brother Ernesto. Sezze is a small place, at the top of a mountain, and it was cool and peaceful there now. I stepped out of the car and placed my hand on the bonnet to feel how hot the engine still was. It had driven us hundreds of miles from France, and I was stiff and tired now.

Amalia was kind. She tried to compensate for our lack of communication by smiling. All that summer she cooked for us.

Claudio was very solicitous. Every morning he fed me oranges, telling me they would do me good.

I suffered from the high temperatures. I was also suffering terrible morning sickness. It lasted all day, and I was throwing up regularly. Much of the time I was subdued and tired, from the sickness, the heat, and anxiety. Some of the time I was able to block out thoughts of the future, but at others, my fears crowded in on me.

Life in Italy passed uneventfully enough. Claudio introduced me to his nephews, they were called Roberto and Mauro, and they were 8 and 10. I didn't care much for Roberto, a skinny boy who kept an unhappy collection of birds in cages behind the house. But Mauro was more likeable, chubby, open, and smiling. They often accompanied us on our little outings, the chief attraction being Claudio's car.

I became fond of Amalia, though I could not say much to her. I spent a lot of time with her in her kitchen, eating her food or watching her prepare it. Tomatoes on everything. Mountains of warm pasta at every meal. Olive oil lacing each dish. Black and green olives with bread. Crispy chicken drumsticks. Red and green pepper sliced and cooked over a wood fire. When I was very sick, she would grow concerned and concoct a herb tea for me, but I found them horrible to drink so they didn't help much.

Our chief amusement was to get in the car and drive to visit some friend or cousin that Claudio hadn't seen for a while. When we got there it was always the same ritual. They would nod and smile at me and put the little pot of coffee on the stove to make Espresso. I noted how tidy and clean their houses were, with no clutter or ornaments to impede their daily dusting. Sometimes, if we were in a house with a garden, we would sit outside. There were always big baskets of figs that had fallen off the trees, and people would lazily eat away at them.

Latina seemed to be a very abundant land, with tomatoes and melons growing copiously in every field you looked at and it seemed a very healthy sort of life. But I missed Dublin and my friends, and the fun of the pubs and the banter in my own language.

Chapter 22

AWAY FROM DUBLIN, I realised that I really did not know Claudio. Against this foreign backdrop, he seemed as alien as the dry Italian landscape. The intense heat sickened me and heightened my morning sickness. I quickly ran out of books to read, having only brought two novels with me, and I lay around in Claudio's little flat, too sick to do much. The flat was small and seemed airless in this heat. It was a conversion at the top of the old farmhouse where he had grown up.

As the day progressed the heat would rise until, at times, I felt I would suffocate in the little rooms. Claudio's lifestyle was modest compared to what his hyperbolic speeches had led me to believe. His furniture was mismatched, and he seemed to have few possessions. The old double bed was ancient, and the bedlinen was frayed and faded. There was a big wardrobe full of his old clothes. I used to take them out and ask him about them, and when he used to wear them. There were flared trousers and brightly coloured wide ties from the seventies, shirts with huge collars, and polyester jackets. He shrugged and said that he had never got round to throwing them away.

"My friends are saying what a lazy girlfriend I have got," said Claudio one afternoon when I complained that I was bored. I asked him why. "Because you have been here 3 weeks, Anna, and you have not cleaned the flat one tiny bit."

I was annoyed that they expected me to clean his flat. It was none of my business. Most of the time I felt very sick, and when I wasn't throwing up, I was just tired and wanted to sit around and stay in the shade away from the burning August sunshine.

"You should clean your flat yourself," I told him. He laughed, but there was a glint of amber in his dark brown eyes, and I felt a twinge of anxiety because I had noticed that this only happened when something or someone made him angry. He, in any case, was thoroughly enjoying his holiday. He slept late every morning, and then sang about the kitchen while he prepared his Lavazza coffee. I liked the smell, but I couldn't bear to drink it.

He was delighted to be able to eat Italian food all the time and liked to gorge himself. A peculiar treat for him was to collect lots of green Italian tomatoes and chop them up, put them in a huge plastic basin, mix them with olive oil and salt, and then eat the whole lot. The tomatoes here were a different shape to the ones I was used to. Instead of being round they were sort of long. They tasted good, but I couldn't understand how he could put away the quantities that he did. Needless to say, it wasn't long before his excesses began to show.

"I will have to go to the dressmaker, my trousers are too small," he said, one morning, when I caught him puffing and panting as he tried to fasten the waistband on his trousers. Amalia laughed when he told her, "Porco!" she said. Mauro and Roberto got excited and ran around the kitchen crying out "Porco! Porco!" until she got annoyed and made them be quiet.

That afternoon Claudio and I got in his car, and he drove us to Sezze Romano, to have his trousers altered. He brought three pairs with him. It was a welcome change to leave the village of Sezze behind for a bit. Although Sezze Romano was small, it was recognisably a town. The tall old buildings and narrow streets meant there was welcome shade. Claudio told me proudly that his hometown pre-dated Rome by hundreds of years. Looking round me, I could believe it.

At last, we found the little man who did Claudio's alterations. The business premises were very old, and quite simple. It was a very basic floor – concrete or something, but the old man, immaculate and tidy in white shirt and brown trousers, greeted Claudio effusively. Then he got his wife to come out and say hello to him. I was introduced briefly and then stood, feeling awkward, while they gabbled away. The old man smiled at me while speaking to Claudio, and I didn't trust what he was saying. Eventually, Claudio gave him the trousers to be altered and we left.

"He says he has a daughter if I want to get married!" laughed Claudio. I didn't think this was very funny.

"Why can't she choose a boyfriend herself?" I asked him but Claudio explained that was how it was here.

"They don't really like me," he said. "But to them, I seem rich, they see my big car, and they think I have money," he explained.

I thought how old-fashioned it was, but I had already realised that it was like that here, under the sunshine and smiles was an obsession with money, and a strangely formal code of behaviour that I simply was not used to. I told Claudio I was glad that I came from a society where women chose their own partners.

"Yes! "he agreed. "Then when it goes wrong, you can only blame yourself!"

Chapter 23

THAT EVENING WE HAD a visitor. Claudio's sister Fernanda came to visit Amalia and I was introduced with great importance as Claudio's pregnant girlfriend. Fernanda was round and blonde, totally unlike all her brothers. She was jolly and laughed a lot. She hugged me and made me welcome.

I sat at the table in Amalia's cool, clean marble kitchen and nodded and smiled as the two of them spoke to each other and tried to include me. As usual, Amalia was cooking. This was to be the evening meal. The kitchen was full of good smells – the tomato sauce simmering on the hob, the chicken cooking in the oven. The smell of garlic wafted over us and for the first time that day I felt the desire to eat something as my nausea had passed leaving me ravenous.

But the next day, my nausea had returned and I wondered why it was called morning sickness as it lasted most of the day. I threw up twice that morning and told Claudio I didn't feel well enough to leave his flat, but he told me to stop being silly and we walked the short distance to Ernesto and Amalia's. Claudio never walked anywhere if he could help it, but I suppose he was afraid I would vomit in his shiny new car. He had swapped his lovely Alfa Romeo for a big black BMW. I mourned the Alfa Romeo, somehow the BMW had none of its glamour.

Back in Amalia's house, I was withdrawn and quieter than usual. I was fed up. I still felt sick and out of sorts, and a terrible kind of despair filled me when I thought about the situation I was in. I couldn't find the energy to be polite any longer, to smile and try to make sense of the Italian language I couldn't understand or have a conversation in. I stood up and went out of the kitchen.

Blindly, I pushed open the door of some room and was relieved to see there was a bed there. I lay down on it and let my tears fall. I had no idea how I was going to cope with it every day. Despite everyone's kindness to me, nothing felt familiar to me and I was so homesick for my own student life in Dublin. What was I going to do with a baby? I found it hard being with Claudio all the time. The idea of spending the rest of my life with him seemed daunting to say the least.

I heard the anxious murmurings of Amalia and Fernanda approaching and there they were, standing over me, exclaiming in hushed voices at my tears. Amalia sat down on the bed next to me, her kind brown eyes full of concern, she stroked my arm. Fernanda shook her head sadly, saying I was too young, "E troppo giovane!" I knew she thought Claudio and I an ill-matched couple. I knew I wasn't equal to the predicament I was in. But what could I do?

The two of them left me and went back into the kitchen. About fifteen minutes later, Amalia returned with a herbal tea she had concocted. It didn't smell very appetising when she handed it to me but I sniffed it and sipped at it gingerly. It was very bitter and I didn't want to drink it, but Amalia encouraged me, telling me it would make my stomach feel better. I drank it in the hope that it would relieve my nausea and I managed to swallow about half of it.

When I had finished drinking from the cup, Amalia took it from me, and the two of us just sat in the cool, quiet room. I asked Amalia if she had been sick when she was pregnant, she nodded, but added "not as much as you."

The men's voices were audible from the kitchen and Fernanda's frequent spirited interjections. Amalia and I giggled as we listened to her scolding the men, disagreeing with something they said.

Chapter 24

A FEW DAYS LATER, we met up with another couple, Gioberto and Debbie, who were from Manchester. Gioberto worked for Claudio's nephew. They had come on holiday to Rome, and they wanted Claudio to show them round. One evening, they joined us in Sezze and the four of us went down into the village to have ice cream. In Italy, no one went to the pub, they just went to cafes or ice cream parlours.

I was feeling content that evening because for once I was not feeling sick, and it was nice and cool. Also, although I didn't have much in common with Debbie, it was a great relief to have someone I could talk to in English. She was a tall, slim girl, with dyed blonde hair in a stylish short cut. She wore a lot of carefully applied eye make-up, and white jeans with a vivid pink, tight-fitting t-shirt. In the little Italian village she stood out a mile, and women in the street turned to look at her. I thought it was funny, but she seemed to take it very seriously and she walked carefully along with a curiously self-conscious swing of her hips.

As we entered the ice cream parlour, a small group of people who had finished, stood up to leave. There was a tall, handsome man at their helm, and as he passed my way I instinctively looked at him and half-smiled. When we sat down, I quickly realised that I had made Claudio angry. Although he carried on talking to Debbie and Gioberto, there was a tense undercurrent, and that evening, when we got back to the flat he told me how angry he was with me for smiling at the man in the ice cream parlour. I could not believe it.

"But it didn't mean anything, Claudio," I reasoned. "I was just acknowledging him." But Claudio insisted.

In Italy, he explained, if you look directly into a stranger's eyes like that, it can be misunderstood, it can mean you are giving them the come-on.

"Don't do that again when we are out together. You showed me up in front of our friends," he said.

I continued to try and reason with him, but it was no use. In the end, I was reduced to tears. I left him and went and lay down on the double bed in his room. A sudden frightening loneliness came over me as I lay there in the close little room. Here I was, in an unfamiliar country I didn't particularly care for, pregnant by a man I barely knew and seemed to have little in common with. I lay there, trying to be calm. The warm scented night air floated over me in eddies, and the curtains at the window billowed gently in and out. I listened to the quiet rustling sound they made, and I felt soothed.

At least I didn't feel sick. Soon I drifted off to sleep. After a while, I felt Claudio getting into the bed next to me. He kissed me gently and slowly on my neck before going to sleep himself.

The next day we drove into Rome to meet Gioberto and Debbie. As usual, it was too hot for me. Twice on the way down the winding hillside from Sezze to Latina, Claudio had to stop the car and pull over onto the side of the road so that I could be sick. He was losing patience now and said he would take me to a doctor and get some tests done. He didn't think it was normal to be this sick for so long.

When we got to Rome we parked the car and met up with Gioberto and Debbie. They were wearing sunglasses and shorts and carrying guidebooks. Despite being Italian, Gioberto managed to look as English as Debbie, perhaps it was his clothes. They both had enormous sunglasses on. The city was beautiful, but I wasn't in the right frame of mind to enjoy it. The endless walking around exhausted me, and when we got to St Peter's I was secretly pleased when we were turned away because Debbie was in shorts. Women must be covered up in order to enter. Claudio was annoyed and tried to remonstrate, but the security guard, or whoever he was, would have none of it. Debbie felt bad. "I'm so sorry," she murmured. "I should have realised."

I told her not to worry. Claudio however, was off on a tirade against the Catholic church. I had realised that he and his family were very anti-clerical. He said that the Catholic church was rotten to the core, that it had too much power and that people were stupid to let them tell them what to do. "But at least here it is not so bad as in Ireland."

I baulked at the insult to my country and said so. It could have turned into another argument, and as we had just gotten over the ice cream parlour incident, I decided to cool it. However, I notched it up as another sign of our incompatibility and I worried about it in private.

I don't remember much else about the day. But that evening, on the drive back to Sezze, the skies suddenly darkened and it began to rain very heavily. I was absolutely delighted. I made Claudio stop the car and I ran out into the rain, holding my arms out as if I wanted to hug it. He told me I was mad and to get back in the car. I got back in, my clothes already wet. But I was glad. For the first time in weeks, I felt refreshed and cool.

After a few more weeks, my sickness subsided and I began to feel better. With the improvement in my health came impatience to get back to my real life, to Dublin. I kept a tally of the days until the start of term in an old notebook I had brought with me. Claudio laughed, but he told me he was in no hurry to return to Dublin and earn money.

We had some good times. In the evenings, we all sat out in the courtyard under the vine leaves and ate Amalia's lovely food and I listened to them talk. They drank red wine with their meals, but I refrained, thinking it would be bad for the pregnancy. I was now plagued with fears that there would be something wrong with the baby.

The days went by and I grew more restless. I was impatient now to leave Italy. It was late afternoon when we left Sezze, descending for the last time to flat Latina via the curly mountain road that I dreaded when he had been drinking too much wine. When we reached Rome, he put on a cassette of Claudio Baglioni and we both sang along.

That night we stopped off in Firenze and slept in a tiny hotel. The heat was stifling and we both had to keep getting out of bed to dampen towels with cold water and spread them over ourselves so that we could keep cool.

I was tired by now of the unrelenting heat and when at last we crossed the Italian border into Switzerland it began to rain. I was excited as a child on Christmas morning and put the car windows down so that I could feel the blessed drops and smell the rain. Claudio was happy too because I was revived and myself again.

When we got to France, I was amused to see large posters everywhere, proclaiming "La France a besoin d'enfants". It seemed the government was worried about the falling birth rate in France and had launched a campaign to encourage people to have more children. The posters had big photos of beautiful babies, with captions which said things like: "There's more to life than sex!"

I pointed them out to Claudio and translated them for him. He laughed ruefully and said, "We do our bit for France, eh, Anna?" But I knew this baby would not be for France. I would return to Trinity soon to complete my degree, and my baby would be born in Dublin. The idea pleased me.

I was buoyed up by happiness, by my hopes for the future and love of this dashing, unpredictable man. My life seemed all before me.

Chapter 25

My sister Margaret sat on my bed chewing her nails.

"What on earth are you going to do?" she asked.

I explained that Claudio was going on ahead to Dublin to get us a flat. He would continue working and I would continue attending college. It was my final year.

"When are you going to tell Mum and Dad?"

We were both dreading this.

"I have another check up with the doctor in four days. I'll tell them when I've had that."

My sister stared at my abdomen in fear.

"You're really showing," she said. "I wouldn't be surprised if Mum copped on without you having to tell her."

Strangely, Mum didn't notice. However, my lethargy and silences got on her nerves.

"Surely you're not napping in the afternoon at your age?" she asked me when she found me lying on my bed one afternoon.

I was feeling exhausted. The heat that summer in Alsace was terrible, and I felt worse because the place was totally landlocked. At least in Italy Claudio could drive to the coast for us to be near water. But here we were miles and miles away from the sea. I longed for damp old Dublin, and the cool shadows which I now knew were my natural habitat.

I tried to keep out of Mum's way. Only a few more weeks and I could leave France, get back to Dublin, and be with Claudio. I felt anxious away from him.

The day of my check-up arrived, my sister came with me. I liked my gynaecologist, Dr Keim, a small, lively man with glasses, who did not seem shocked that I was not married. He looked me over, examined me and then stood back.

"You look much bigger than you should" he said. "Let's do an ultrasound to see what's going on."

I began to panic. What if my worst fears were confirmed, and there was something wrong with the baby? I felt very anxious as he covered my abdomen in cold jelly and began to press on it with an ultrasound probe.

He stared intently at the screen while slowly moving the probe. The room seemed very tense. Then he gave a little chuckle.

"Mademoiselle, it's not one baby – it's two! You have little twins in here!" He stood up, looking pleased and excited.

"Shall I tell your sister to come and have a look?"

I was speechless. My sister came in and stared at the screen while Dr Keim chatted about the presence of the twin embryos.

Margaret and I went home by bus and disappeared up to the top of the house for some privacy. I was shell-shocked. The fact it was twins would make it even harder to tell my parents. I did not know it then, but it would make the practicalities of my situation even more difficult. I clutched the printout of the scan and moaned in desperation.

"Oh my God, Margaret, twins! This could only happen to me! Why me? Why me?"

Margaret tried to cheer me up.

"Look at it this way, anyone can have one baby – the fact that it's twins makes it special!"

I was not convinced.

That evening I rang Claudio and told him. He was silent for a second, but then he rallied. He did not seem to think it was a problem. However, I decided not to tell my parents it was twins. It would be bad enough telling them that I was pregnant.

As for their reaction to my news; that's another story. There were no raised voices, no recriminations, just an awful sadness. I would have done anything to make it better for them. But it was a one-way ticket now, and I would just have to hang on and hope for a happy ending.

Chapter 26

BACK IN DUBLIN WITH CLAUDIO, I kept a low profile. I went into college as little as possible and avoided all but my closest friends. I didn't want to discuss my pregnancy and wore a big mulberry coloured cape and kidded myself that no one had noticed. My relationship with Claudio mellowed and I taught myself to cook basic meals to keep him happy.

I still attended college, discreetly turning up to my lectures and seminars. In the evenings I sat in the small, modern house in Sandymount that Claudio had rented for us and mused on the turn of events my life had taken. Now that I was pregnant and we were living together, our relationship had changed. Gone were the heady, adventurous days of our courtship. Now we lived together in this toy house, we went grocery shopping together, we ate meals together, and at the end of the day, we slept together in the little bedroom with its cardboard walls and its white furniture. Life seemed strangely routine and distant. Is this what being a proper adult was like? I felt a nagging doubt inside myself, but damped it down, telling myself that it would all make sense once the babies arrived.

Now it was evening and I sat alone in the little, clutter-free sitting room.

Strangely, Claudio had gone out attired in a red jogging suit and an old pair of trainers. I had never known him to jog before. I got up and pulled back the curtains to look out of the window. There was a team of girls outside in the back field, playing hockey. Their cries rose in muffled waves through the dusk. I thought of Claudio, jogging around the field, trying to get a look at the girls. How silly he would look to them. He would be panting too, for he was out of condition. He never walked anywhere if he could drive. I sat back down and picked up my dog-eared copy of Yeats.

Soon, Claudio would be back insisting I put down my book and pay him some attention or watch a film with him. We would watch some noisy action film where men blew each other's heads off with automatic weapons or chased each other across the screen in endless, boring car chases.

When forced to watch these movies, my mind went into a kind of numb daze. I simply could not make any sense of them. There seemed to be no plot, no point to them.

I was disappointed to find that whereas dating Claudio had been exciting and fun, living with him wasn't. For a start, I was pregnant, and now that I was showing, he didn't seem keen to be seen out with me. Secondly, I wasn't as free to spend time with my friends and thirdly, he expected proper meals. Even though he realised I couldn't cook, he expected me to go to the supermarket with him, to help him prepare the meals and to wash up afterwards.

This sensible routine didn't suit me at all. Sometimes, I just wanted to have a bowl of soup or a bag of crisps and read. But Claudio would get impatient. He hated me to eat crisps, so I used to hide them in the airing cupboard at the top of the stairs and eat them when he wasn't around. Every morning he would cut up an orange and make me eat it.

"Go on, it's good for you, Anna, good for the bebbies!"

I would eat it to pacify him. I admit my diet wasn't great. I suppose I had a haphazard approach to food and didn't take it that seriously. I wasn't ready to stop being a student, and this was reflected in my slapdash attitude to meals. It drove him crazy.

"An Italian woman, she will spend all day making a nice sauce for the family!" he would tell me. "But you, Anna, you spend ten minutes in the kitchen!"

I had little intention of changing my ways, and anything I did was merely a token gesture. Privately, I had not been impressed by the Italian women I had met and thought they should get a life. But any criticism of his homeland made Claudio angry, so I didn't say anything. There was simply no point. We seldom argued now. It was a truce.

Chapter 27

ONE TUESDAY NIGHT IN deep winter, I went into labour. I got what I thought was a very bad stitch in my side while I was sitting watching television with Claudio. At first, I said nothing, thinking it would pass, but the pain kept recurring, very sharp. By the time we went to bed, I had what I thought was bad stomach cramp. I remember my nightie was getting all wet and my knickers, and I couldn't understand it. I thought I was wetting myself so I got out of bed and went to the loo. My waters had broken and I didn't have a clue what was happening. I had read the books about what to expect, but I mustn't have taken a thing in. I was actually sitting there pushing like mad.

By now the cramps were getting really bad and I was soaking so I had to face the fact that something was up. I went back in to Claudio. "Claudio," I said, "I think something must be wrong."

Well, he acted as if I had electrocuted him. He jumped out of the bed with amazing speed. I couldn't believe my time had come. I was a month early, and mentally unprepared. I had only attended one ante-natal class in Holles Street Hospital, and it was just a preliminary one where they handed out leaflets. Nothing about breathing or pain or anything.

Claudio panicked but he did manage to find the hospital telephone number and soon I was talking to a nurse telling her what was happening to me. She said, "your waters have broken, you'd better get in here straight away."

I was shaking. My teeth were chattering and my hands had gone icy. I was terrified. So this was it. I couldn't grasp it. I just was not ready. I pulled some loose clothes on and Claudio drove like mad to Holles Street Hospital. By the time we got there, I was soaking and the cramps were really bad. I kept on praying that it was a false alarm. "Please God, not now, not yet." I was dead tired as I had been doing a lot of running around for essay deadlines, lectures, etc.

We went into the hospital and were told to go up a few floors. It was a really old-fashioned lift where you had to close the grille and wait before it got started. Claudio was having a fit. Soon, I was in a room where a couple of nurses took over and tried to time my contractions. I was really panicking. The pains were getting terrible and there seemed to be no time between them to get my breath. I kept saying "I can't stand it. I can't stand it."

I felt doomed, like Patrick Pearse before he faced the death squad, or Jesus sweating it out in the Garden of Gethsemane, surrounded by useless people who couldn't help. Only I could do this. I felt really alone. Then the nurses decided they would have to monitor the babies' heartbeats. They started trying to harness me up in some bloody contraption; a foetal monitor which was a big belt thing. I couldn't bear anyone to touch my abdomen. I asked them please not to. But they ignored me. Eventually, one of them looked at me sternly and said, "we have to check on the babies, after all, they're the most important thing."

I felt like she had slapped me in the face. I wanted to weep but I was way beyond tears, my fear was enormous. I don't know how long I was there, but eventually someone came down from the delivery ward and told us there was room for me now. I felt like I had been sentenced. They took me upstairs. They asked me did I want Claudio with me. I said no way. He was absolutely useless, no comfort at all. He probably thought it was no big deal – every woman does it. When I tried to tell him how awful it felt he just looked completely detached and sort of smug, as if to say, "I'm glad it's not me." I almost hated him at that point. I asked them for something to kill the pain but they said it was too soon.

They asked me did I need to go to the bathroom as this was my last chance. It was like any last requests. I went in. A woman was throwing up in the next toilet. I saw her come out, ashen faced. She looked about 50 but I found out the next day that she was only 31. She delivered a baby boy two hours before me.

The delivery room had about six or eight beds in it. All the beds seemed to have groaning, sweating women on them. People are shocked by this when I tell them, but actually it didn't frighten me in the slightest. I was locked in my own tight capsule of pain, and if anything, I found it reassuring to have other women in the same situation around me.

They had given me a white dress thing instead of my clothes. I lay down on the bed. It was just more of the same. The pain intensifying. I kept on and on asking for something, anything to deaden it and after ages and ages, they gave me pethidine. They had given me this young nurse who was supposed to hold my hand through it all, talk me through it. She wasn't much older than me, and very earnest, but her impervious calm was no comfort to me. "Have you ever had a baby yourself?" I asked her. When she said no, I felt completely hopeless. I dropped her hand.

I was sweating by now, and no matter what position I lay in nothing alleviated the pain. I begged her to get me a cold wet cloth to put on my forehead as I was burning up. I remember I had to insist before she did this. It was lovely and cool for a minute or two and then it heated up, she wasn't too quick about freshening it up for me. I think I asked for a drink of water as well. I kept panicking and wanting to scream. They told me to control myself. That there were other women in worse pain than me and that my yells would upset them. I think they had to be strict with us as we were a hair's breadth from insanity.

At last, the pethidine began to make me drowsy. I wished the lights were not so bright. I closed my eyes and longed for quiet and darkness. The room was ugly and bright white. There was nothing restful about it. Up to this point they had been telling me not to push but now they started telling me to push. I had been watching the big white-faced clock on the wall all the time. The hands seemed glued to it. I would look at it expecting time to have gone by, and maybe ten minutes would have gone. I kept on asking them "How much longer? How much longer?" They gave me evasive answers that filled me with despair. They said, "a few hours." I said, "I can't last that long, I just can't last it out." They said, "you will, you will, you can do it, you're doing great. Think of the babies."

Think of the babies? What babies? The pain obliterated everything, and I had even forgotten why I was there. I told the midwife that I wanted to die and begged for a caesarean. They told me it's too late. I panicked.

The feeling of pressure was unbearable. Like someone had planted a bomb inside me and I was going to explode. I could not believe that I had to push this out through my vagina. It seemed impossible, barbaric, a cruel joke. I could not believe that we could send people to the moon, and still no way had been found to make this easier. I wanted to throw up. I protested. They insisted. The midwife was imploring me, losing her cool. I asked when Dr Murphy, my consultant would be here, but they kept saying it wasn't time yet. The young doctor in charge was anxious. I could tell he had never delivered twins before.

At last, my consultant was called. Claudio had paid extra, and for that I am eternally grateful. I knew then that it was nearly the end. The worst was yet to come, but at last it would be over. He came in, wearing a white coat. I had total confidence in him because I knew he had delivered four of my cousins. He saw the state I was in. He put his hand on my forehead.

"Ssh," he said. "You'll be alright now. It'll be over soon."

He was totally calm, I felt like Jesus Christ had walked in. The doctor and the midwife were as relieved as I was to see him. He began at once to move very quickly, giving instructions rapidly in a quiet voice. I was going mad. I couldn't bear to push, I was ripping apart. "Don't make me do it, please don't make me," I said. The midwife leant forward urgently and said "Mrs Burdish, please try to push. Your babies are ready to be born. It's very important now not to waste any time."

I knew then that it was up to me. That if I screwed up, the consequences would be dire. They made me lie on my side. I pushed. I heard the midwife say, "I think there's a little hand in the way." She must have pushed it back in. They were trying to get the head. She told me they could see the head. So there really was a baby in there! I kept on pushing till I thought I would die. I hoped it was a son, a boy, so he would never have to go through this or anything like it. "Push, push, you're nearly there!" Their voices were rising in crescendo.

Then Dr Murphy said, "Mrs Burdish, you have a little girl." He held her up then, so I could see her. I gazed in wonderment at this little stranger that had come out of me. She seemed to be asleep, and she looked totally peaceful. Her little fingers were splayed out. Then she opened her eyes and looked at me.

After that it wasn't as hard to push the second baby out, another girl.

When it was over, I felt rather pleased with myself. I refused to get into the wheelchair they brought for me and insisted on walking back to the ward. This turned out to be foolish as I promptly haemorrhaged all over the floor. I apologised to the young nurse who had to clean it up, but she was very kind and only smiled at me.

Chapter 28

AT VISITING TIME, THE ward filled up with subdued looking husbands. The girl in the very last bed whose baby had no official father, sat holding her daughter and looking ahead defiantly. Since having her baby four days ago, her only visitors were her two flatmates who wanted to hear all the gory details and then left her.

Claudio appeared looking fit and well, his swarthy face as startling and good looking as ever. I looked at him with wonderment, marvelling at his regular features, his Latin glamour, wondering at the huge difference in our appearances. He was dark and brown-eyed, I was fair and blue-eyed, he was short and I was tall. I reminded myself that this was the father of my children. His children. His babies had grown inside me. How strange it all was.

He looked out of place in this ward, among all these beds of wan, quiet women in their unglamorous dressing gowns. He wore his navy cashmere coat and carried an enormous basket overflowing with the most gorgeous flower arrangement. As he approached my bed, the scent of his cologne reached me, and I felt awkward and ashamed that I was not wearing any make-up.

He saw my listless expression. "What's wrong with you, Anna?" he said.

I felt angry and disappointed at my own lack of enthusiasm. I knew that to show the merest hint of disenchantment with any facet of the baby-making process was social suicide in Ireland.

He walked over to the little cots next to my bed where our daughters lay. "A pity the second one wasn't a son," he said then, regretfully.

A pain sharp as a knife went through me. So this was all he could say after all my trouble! It came to me then in one bitter flash how quickly he had bundled me off into the delivery room and how, after the birth, he had not bothered to accompany me back to my bed. Resentment lodged in my gullet like bile. There were no words for any of this.

How had I fallen into this trap? Looking back, it seemed as though my whole education had been a long-drawn-out warning against men and the harm they would inflict on me if I allowed them near me. In the end, it was as though I had embraced my own destruction.

I knew that he was trying hard to do all the right things. The flowers, the new slippers in their Brown Thomas bag..... but yet, he disappointed me.

"What are we going to do?" I asked him.

"We will have to go back to Italy for a while." He didn't look at me as he spoke, because he knew what I would think of that idea.

"Oh, go where you like!" I snapped. "But I am not going back to Italy."

I felt a wicked desire to torment him. What right had he to sit there, bronzed and gorgeous, while I lay here torn and bruised. I knew he was shocked at the change in my appearance, that I now looked very different to the glowing girl he had taken to the Powerscourt Gardens in the summer. I felt that I was now a completely different person, half the person that I used to be, and I blamed him.

At once he was all a-flutter trying to appease me.

"Okay, darling, we can talk about these things later. Don't be like this, Anna. What have I done to you?"

I just sat with my face in stoney profile to him. What was wrong? I didn't know. I just felt emptied out, and bitter. I grasped at the threads of my anger to escape the apathy that I could sense in the pit of my stomach, the apathy that I dreaded.

After he'd gone I called for one of the nurses and asked her to bring me the biggest vase she could find for the bouquet. They were, after all, probably the most beautiful flowers I would ever receive in my life.

Chapter 29

OUT ON LOWER MOUNT Street two girls are walking leisurely, books under their arms, talking and laughing. Where are they going on this dull February day? Grafton Street? Bewleys Café maybe, or a walk round Brown Thomas? I used to be like them. I am a mother now. I have been torn apart like a fox by hungry hounds and put back together somehow. How quiet I feel. How determined. I am on my second life. I have gained something but lost something also. It is as if I had left my old self in the labour ward, to be cleared up with the debris of the birth.

Family tell me that my grandmother refused to see either her baby or her husband for two whole days after the birth. Now I understand her fury, her feelings of betrayal, but who can we blame but the one who made us?

I suppose I am one of those women who never really knows what she wants. I get rushes of decision, I have periods of great austerity, marking my diary with purposeful lists and tasks that must be done. I make appointments with the dentist, get shoes heeled and peel spuds for supper. The place is littered with my manic lists. Lists of do's, don'ts, maybes, intentions, dislikes and likes but my desires and aims are constantly in flux. This applies especially to matters of the heart.

How could any man live with me? It isn't a man I want at all but some great God. I am forever longing to find a man so I can place him on a great pedestal. Disappointment makes me cruel. I cannot bear it. Gods with clay feet make me want to break them.

In the old-fashioned hospital theatre, they lectured us after the birth. The seats were wooden and very uncomfortable. My stitches still hurt and I squirmed on the hard bench. The room was dark and severe and looked out onto the back of Pearse Street. A humdrum sight on a bleak February afternoon. They droned on about methods of contraception, but as we are in Ireland they dare not mention the coil, the pill, or even condoms. They whitter on about 'the safe period'. I switch off. Outside the grey day seemed to mock my memories of sun and love and glamour. In this grey winter light, Dublin sprawled in barren unloveliness and like myself, the city I loved, the city I had seen revealed in all her glory, was now unrecognisable.

****

Once it was all over and the babies were safe in the neo-natal unit, there was only one person in the world I really wanted to see; my mother.

She got a plane from France as soon as she could and arrived at the hospital laden with baby clothes and cot blankets. Her face was shining. She had been to look at the twins even before she came to the ward to see me.

"Oh Anna," she said. "They are beautiful." I was so grateful for her loving words that I burst into tears.

Just as well my mother was so enthusiastic as I would rely on her heavily from now on.

Once out of hospital I realised I could not manage two babies by myself, and Claudio had very little confidence around them. He was also keen to get back to work as the bills still needed to be paid. I could see he was beginning to panic.

It was decided that I should go back to Mulhouse with my mum, taking the twins with me, and wait a few months while Claudio got a home together for us in England. He had cousins in Manchester and he could get work there. I was very disappointed. "But I always thought we would stay in Dublin!" I said. Claudio said no and that it was too difficult for him to make a living here in Dublin.

We had to wait until the twins were six weeks old before we could take them on a plane. Mum and I, each carrying a baby, flew back to France where dad picked us up and took us to the house in Mulhouse. Claudio went back to England to try and sort something out for us. It was all so rushed I did not have time to be sorry about leaving the little house in Sandymount. It had never felt very real to me anyhow.

After a while, Claudio came to Mulhouse to visit us.

I told him I would marry him. When he had left, shiny and expansive with pleasure, I murmured the word 'husband' to myself over and over. I conjured up his image in my mind as I repeated the word to myself. It had indeed a magical quality. It meant forever and ever. I looked at my babies and realised that if I married their father now, they need never know the uncertain beginnings of our partnership. Above all, I would not have to be indebted to my parents for their support. I would have my own house and be in charge of my life.

I went into town and walked around the department stores reminding myself how I would have my husband's money now, and not have to ask my parents for everything. I spent some time in the hardware section comparing sets of crockery.

I felt strange. Everything would have to be done at once. Nothing had preceded all of this. My life had burgeoned way out of my control.

Outside in the streets, I noticed men all around. A tall, gaunt man with dark hair passed me by. A fine man, I found myself thinking. What fine children he would make. A stab of doubt assailed me then. A new fear formed itself. A large part of my freedom had gone. Married, I would no longer be free to look at men in town, to trail my gaze in cafes or crowded bars, to dream, or to fantasise. The doubt inside me strengthened and became panic. There was too much I had not seen and tried. I had had no time, no time at all! How could I promise Claudio the rest of my life! The prospect terrified me. Forever and ever! The years stretched away ahead of me.

I returned home, shaken. I could not go through with it but yet the thought of backing out brought me out in a cold sweat. The disappointment of my family, my continued absolute and indefinite dependence on them.

I reminded myself I was a mother. It was too late to retract now. How many times had I not given myself to him? In hotel rooms and between the linen sheets in the old-fashioned bed in his Italian hometown. I remembered his caresses, his murmured words of encouragement, desire. He was my first. I could never replace him. The other men were only phantoms. Between us we had produced two flesh and blood children.

And yet all the promises of youth rushed to my throat to gag me.

My freedom was gone.

Chapter 30

It was the hardest thing in the world when I told Claudio I could not marry him.

He did not argue. His silence was proof of his shock.

He said he would go.

"There's no need to go yet," I said, uselessly. The blow could not be softened.

The weather was atrocious, thick unrelenting snow lay a foot thick over Europe. It was minus 18. I could not bear to think of him driving back over the Alps.

"I'll say goodbye to the bebbies," he said then. He already had his navy cashmere coat on. I stood at the door of our daughters' bedroom and he went over to each cot in turn. The little girls blew bubbles and gurgled up at him, sublimely unaware. I wished I could fade away. I knew that my parents would take care of them.

At first, he spoke to them in a low voice, in Italian, then leant over and kissed them. He turned then, abruptly, and brushed past me as he left the room.

I glimpsed his face and saw my own pain. I knew that if he were to survive, he would have to steel his heart, seal it up against us.

Outside there was nothing but dead winter and the endless snow, silently falling.

Chapter 31

I SPENT A YEAR in Mulhouse, in my parents' house, looking after the twins with the help of my mother. I continued to pursue my degree by correspondence, reading and doing essays while the babies slept. I realised too late that I had lost my life in Dublin. I couldn't get used to it.

Torn away from the city I loved I lived in a state of perpetual and acute homesickness. If you have never experienced homesickness, you will think nothing of my suffering, but it is the most horrible feeling. My heart ached constantly and I had the constant feeling that nothing I did mattered, as I was in the wrong place anyway. I lived in a state of suspended animation. I missed my friends, Dublin, Kielty, and my freedom. But the babies had to come first. Here, with my parents, they had a comfortable home, stability, and the love and care of my mother who was as good as a Norland nanny. I don't know how she managed it, but my babies slept like clockwork, and they grew and gained weight without any problem.

Out of the blue, my father's sister Agnes arrived from London to stay for a few weeks. She, unlike me, was a tremendous Francophile. She had done a French degree and all things French were wonderful to her. She felt about all things French the way I felt about all things Irish.

She was in Strasbourg doing some research on the 'Malgré Nous'. The 'Malgré Nous', or 'Despite Ourselves' was the name of an unfortunate group of Alsatian men who were forced to fight for the Germans during the Second World War.

Although I felt uprooted and unable to connect with anyone in a real sense, when Aunt Agnes spoke about the dislocated past of this part of France, so frequently swapped like an inanimate parcel between the French and the Germans, with all the resultant problems of identity and conflicted loyalties, I did feel a lot of sympathy. Ireland's history was terrible, but at least we had kept our identity, and questions of loyalty were usually clear-cut. Here in central Europe, where frontiers and boundaries were more fluid, it wasn't so easy for people to know who they were, or to defend their borders.

We lived in a neighbourhood not far from the centre of Mulhouse, it was called Riedisheim. It wasn't a bad house. It was big, and the rooms were spacious, but it was quite dark in winter, and at times I felt it had a brooding atmosphere. It didn't help matters when we heard that a Jewish family had lived there in the Second World War and that someone local had denounced them to the authorities. Then they were taken away.

Across the road, in another old house, lived three old sisters. Every time I took the twins out in the unwieldy double buggy, one or other of them would lean out of the window and call out "Bonjour!" Then they would congratulate me on the healthiness of my daughters, and smile and say "Eh! C'est du travail! C'est du travail!" I would agree, and smile and continue with my walk.

My aunt would go over and talk to them about the war. She took a tape recorder with her and recorded the conversations. She said they could fill her in on the local history that would be useful for her research. She went over several times, but I think in the end one of the old ladies got too tired, or upset, and said she didn't want to remember anymore. So that was that.

Then one day Agnes said she was going to Colmar and asked me if I wanted to come. I wasn't interested in seeing Colmar, but a day away from Mulhouse and the rigorous routine of nappy changes and bottle feeds did appeal. I left my poor mother in charge of the babies for the day and set off with Agnes for Colmar. I knew it was famous but I wasn't excited. The history of this part of the world seemed dark and dreary to me. It simply did not touch me in any real way. It didn't feel as though it had recovered from the Second World War.

I forget how we got to Colmar. We must have caught the train. Agnes wanted to go to the famous museum called the Musée d'Unterlinden. I was interested at first because I usually like paintings, even though I know next to nothing about art. We spent hours there, walking through countless rooms. I just remember endless pictures with religious themes. Dour-faced Virgins clasped infant Jesuses, who did not resemble a baby in any way, instead they were like creepy little miniature men with grim expressions.

The paintings were, even I could see, beautiful, but I couldn't see any joy in any of them. The endless portrayals of the crucifixion were cruelly realistic, and the overall impression was terribly austere. This was the unsmiling Christianity of cold Northern Europe. There were no round cherubs or consolatory smiles. No, here was the horror of a cold world where suffering and sin were omnipresent. I found it depressing. I noted with disgust there wasn't even a café, but luckily Agnes had enough at last and we went to find a café. I had tried to show enthusiasm, and translated the German titles of some of the paintings as well as I could when she asked me, but she could see I wasn't very enthusiastic.

"Honestly, Anna", she said, as we sipped our drinks. "You've been to university, you should be taking more interest in where you live. This is an interesting part of France. It's saturated in art and history."

I looked at her despondently. For a start, I was pissed off, because of the way they had served me my tea in one of those fiddly little glasses in a little metal holder.

"I dunno, Agnes" I said. "I just don't want to be here."

She began to talk to me. She was very good really. She didn't go on about why I had been daft enough to get pregnant in the first place, and for that I was grateful. At the same time, I was impatient with her. I wasn't interested in living here. I looked down at the miserable little glass full of tea in my hands and wished with all my heart I was in Bewleys in Westmoreland Street, with one of those nice solid little teapots in front of me, and the warm hum of Irish voices around me. I could have wept.

We went back to Mulhouse, and a few days later before Agnes left she bought me some cod-liver oil tablets and told me that I needed counselling. I didn't listen. I knew exactly what I needed. I needed to get the hell out of here.

My father came home from work that evening and I noticed how tired he looked. I remembered that I had gone against him when I insisted on going to Trinity instead of Bristol University. And now I had repaid him by coming home with two more children to provide for. Claudio would not help me now that I had rejected him. That night I was so full of despair that I could barely sleep.

At the bottom of the road where we lived was the little Catholic church where my twins had been baptised. The next morning, as I went through my baby care routine mechanically, I decided to go there and seek advice from the priest. Inside I was breaking up. I needed to speak to someone. But who? I could not burden my mother any further and both my sisters were pursuing their own lives in England. I had no friends here in Mulhouse. In desperation I decided that I would try and get advice from the local Catholic priest. He was a robust and placid man who radiated calm. So I headed off that morning while the babies were napping and my mum was on the phone to a friend.

I knocked on the Presbytery door and waited. Sure enough, Père Beubon's heavy steps could be heard and then he opened the door. He must have been in the middle of his dinner because he was still chewing, but he noticed how upset I was and told me to come in.

We both sat down in the little reception area and he asked me what was troubling me. It all spilled out. My unplanned pregnancy, the failure of my relationship with the father, the burden on my parents and the upset to my whole family. I had no income, no work, and no friends. I was an "étranger" in France, an unenviable position. I was desperate. Maybe it would have been better not to proceed with the pregnancy? I had messed up too many people with this selfish course of action.

Père Beubon had been listening carefully and now he spoke. "Avorter? – Au moins vous n'avez pas fait ça." Abortion? At least you didn't do that.

I pointed out that it did seem awful for everyone at the moment, and maybe I had been misguided. But the big priest shook his head slowly.

"No," he said. "It's hard now, but things will get better. Be glad that you have good parents to help you. Accept their help. It is a good thing that you did not have an abortion."

At his words a tremendous weight slowly slid off my shoulders.

"Are you sure I made the right decision?" I asked him again. I desperately needed reassurance.

"Oui, ma fille." He said.

I thanked him and he blessed me. I got up to leave. At the door he put his hand on my shoulder and told me not to worry too much, and that he would pray for me. Then he said those heartening French words: "Allez, Bon Courage!"

Chapter 32

After my talk with Père Beubon, my mind cleared a bit. I decided that I had to get a home together for myself and my twins. I could not leave my parents to bring them up. There was no future for me in France, I did not have the right papers and I had no desire to stay.

After much discussion with my parents, we reached a compromise. I could go to London, where my sisters were already working and get a job. Once I was established, they would let me take the twins to live with me. I dreaded leaving the babies but I felt I would go mad if I had to keep living like this without any life of my own. I was hopeful that London would offer interesting and well-paid work and that, within a year, I would manage to get a home together for us. I felt tremendous guilt about leaving my mother to mind both babies, but she seemed willing to do it. No doubt she was tired of my angry moods.

So here I was in London, of course. What troubled Irish girl has not tried her powers of survival in the English metropolis? London is full of Irish girls who have had to leave precious things behind, girls with sad faces and a story to tell. London was hard going but by dint of sheer perseverance, I made friends with her streets and gradually she took me under her wing and made it possible for me to survive.

After all, Englishness was not new to me. My father was English, and then there was my time at an English prep school. I still remembered some of those lessons; the wonderful novels of Charlotte and Emily Bronte and the history lessons full of Kings and Queens. Of course, having grown up in Northern Ireland I was familiar with the culture. It was wonderful to have English TV and radio again, and bookshops and pubs. Dublin was off the cards, nobody wanted to hear me going on about it anymore. I had blown it.

Although they are not my people, I like the English. The Irish and English go back a long way. They are like a divorced couple who have had to learn to get along, accept each other's foibles and deformities. Is not nationality, to a certain extent a state of mind, a way of seeing things? We do not always understand each other, but they are mostly kind to me.

I am puzzled and embarrassed. I cannot equate these mild-mannered people with the monstrous armoured cars I used to see bearing down on the little roads of my native province of County Tyrone in Northern Ireland, with the outrages of Bloody Sunday or internment or ugly army checkpoints.

It is not always easy to be Irish in England. When bombs go off, when people die and lives are torn apart I stoop slightly under the weight of a collective guilt. I speak quietly hoping my accent will not offend. My eyes, I am sure, apologise over shop counters as I buy my daily newspaper.

I become a mixture of shame and defiance as I try to reconcile the warring sympathies I house. When I got a job in a big construction firm, I noticed the Irishmen who worked there. Some worked as engineers, others as navvies. Many British people regard the Irish with some affection. They turn to us to remind them of the lighter side of life but there is a flip side to this coin, and it surfaces now and again. We, the far-flung sons and daughters of Ireland, nurse our history like a little deformity. That's Paddy there in the bar, making you laugh, telling you the stories you've come to expect as your due, exaggerating his accent – just what you expect – comforting – good old Paddy!

Out of Ireland have we come. We grow to love our adoptive mother but she can never fully understand us or fully trust us. Holding us at arms' length even after decades – looking at us slightly askance. Our talents are an unexpected bonus. We built her roads, and man her offices but even so, we are not fully trusted.

When bombs go off in Northern Ireland, or on the streets of England's cities, the Irishman is treacherous. His misinterpreted accent is a red rag to a bull, his humour is an insult. Let's make a clown of him.

Bless me, Father, for I have sinned. It is many years since my last confession. Forgive us, mother England, we the sinning Irish, your adopted children, thorns in your flesh. Try to listen to us. Together let us find a cure for your deafness.

One day I was called down to the reception of the big office where I worked to collect a package from a man who had been sent up from the building site. When I got there, I met a quiet middle-aged Irishman. He was waiting patiently, he was very polite as he gave me the package, and though he was in his working clothes, he had a rare kind of dignity, a gentleness. I watched him walk out of the reception area and heard the silly little girls on the desk snigger as they took in his shabby clothes, mimicking his accent. I wished I had found something to say to him. His gentle country voice was still in my ears as I stepped back into the lift, dredging up in my heart all the terrible homesickness I lived with daily. An anger filled me then, a fierce kind of pride. I felt a kind of inexplicable grief. I was glad I was alone in the ill-lit lift, to compose myself.

We are all Irish, I quoted to myself. We are all sons and daughters of Kings. A strange sense of loss filled me.

My digs were typically unglamorous and required just over one-third of my wages. A small room at the top of a cramped family house with a large bed where I stayed for most of every Saturday morning, a chair, and a small functional table. My landlady had a cheerful young daughter and four small dogs who filled the lower half of the house with their unlovely odour. They were not allowed upstairs, thank God, and their access was barred by a wooden board which had been strategically placed across the top of the stairs. As they were fat, they were unable to clamber over it, but on many mornings I snagged my nylons on its rough edges as I rushed out to work.

I lived in Clapham, and I thought it was one of the ugliest places I had ever seen. Its grimy pavements were never scrubbed clean, and its endless collection of grubby little convenience stores and off-licences filled me with gloom. But tonight I was in high spirits because I had a date. I'd met a French gentleman through a friend. His name was Charles and he was keen to talk about home. We were meeting in the lobby of a big hotel in Knightsbridge. It was a balmy summer's evening, and as I entered the lobby I felt a sense of relief.

The plush surroundings lulled my overwrought nerves and erased all thoughts of my monotonous job. The soft carpets, the deft waiters, the large gilt mirrors, and the expensive armchair on which I now sat, all lifted me temporarily into a more lovely world.

The evening expanded as we dined. I had had exactly the right amount of wine and was feeling at peace with the world for the first time in months.

But I couldn't relax. I felt I had to be on my best behaviour. Worst of all, I couldn't eat as much as I wanted because he might peer at me with a slight hint of disapproval, and how could I eat when he was wafting waves of disapproval over me? If there's one thing I've learned to dread, it's male disapproval.

I ordered langoustines as Charles warned me the lobster was not good. When it arrived I had a fit inwardly at the size of the helping. There were about seven or eight curved little langoustines, and me starving! Like a fool I'd been fasting all day in anticipation, intending to gorge myself. I concentrated on not showing my disappointment.

Not that Charles would have noticed. He'd had his aperitif and was beginning to feel all mellow and self-satisfied. The smiley waiters appeared constantly at his elbow, simpering, "Would sir like some more wine? Does sir desire anything more?" I was ashamed for them and buried my nose in my glass.

He began to stroke my hand across the table and I felt mortified.

"Darling, how lovely it is to see you again – how lovely you look," he purred.

The waiters were beginning to smile coyly at me. It dawned on me that they were probably assuming I was having an affair with him. Maybe Charles thought this might happen, but he was a married man with grown-up children.

To hear him talk you'd swear his sons were mouth-wateringly attractive young business dynamos. In fact, it seemed to me that he was forced to devote considerable amounts of his precious time to shunting them around Europe from one expensive educational establishment to another. "They are extravagant!" he sighed. I thought he looked rather tired and was beginning to feel sorry for him as he told me how they had taken over his Kensington flat and run up enormous phone bills.

As he confided in me, I cast a beady eye over the dessert menu, hoping there would be something substantial to fill up the gap, but no, it was one of those places where it's all fiddly little crème caramels or minuscule boules of ice cream. I wondered if the Eight Till Late would still be open when I got back to the flat. When the waiter brought us our coffees, I noted with pleasure the accompanying dish of bonbons. While Charles stirred his coffee, observing that business overall was booming, I selected a nice little number with a nut on the top. Needless to say, as soon as I had it in my mouth he came over all affectionate. I suppose he reckoned it was time, as we were on the coffees.

"You make me feel wonderful." I heard him murmur.

The man had a terrible sense of timing. I tried to look seductive, which was hard as my mouth was full of chocolate. Maybe it was time to cut free from this nonsense.

"Listen, Charles," I said, swallowing my bonbon. "I think there's something you should know. I have two children. They're with my parents in France."

The change in his attitude was instant. He withdrew his hand and leant back in his chair, looking at me. Finally, he said coldly, "I had no idea. I was told you were single."

"I am single" I said. "I didn't marry the father. It wouldn't have worked out."

He was frankly aghast. "But I don't understand... If you knew you couldn't stay with him, why did you go through with it?!"

There wasn't anything more to say really. We ended our meal in a civil manner and went our separate ways. I never heard from him again.

Chapter 33

How had I ended up back in the UK? It was the place I had managed to escape at the age of eighteen when I got my place at Trinity and headed off to Dublin. It seemed a strange quirk of fate that I had ended up back here.

Things hadn't really changed. I liked the buzz and excitement of the city, but I did not really feel part of it. I was full of guilt about the babies I had left behind in France and paralysed by homesickness for Ireland. I found it difficult to make friends with anyone.

There was a handsome Englishman in the big office where I worked. His name was Robert. An Englishman who seemed to come straight from the pages of a Brideshead novel but he was olive-skinned and dark-eyed. He addressed me in his plummy accent and my heart skipped a beat. He must have been a year or two older than me but his face was unlined and unlike me he had no history. He had that unperturbably British confidence, that poise that comes from generations of privilege, of secure identity, that easy solidity that no descendent of Irish immigrants can ever properly attain.

He liked the fact that I was Irish. "I had a girlfriend from Cork once," he told me. He smiled, showing me his even white teeth.

As I struggled with the dreary clerical work I was thankful for his presence in the office. It made it less dull if I could think he might pass by once or twice for a chat. Sometimes he was good-natured. At other times he was restless, bored, and arrogant.

The girl I worked with was a torment. Her name was Samantha.

"My friends call me Sammy," she told me.

She spent most of the day on the phone to her friends. The conversations made my hair stand on end. "What, is she pregnant then?......He's going to marry her?.....How does he know it's his?....."

Her casual malice left me in no doubt that women are their own worst enemy. I tried to keep myself to myself, confiding nothing, repelled by her bitchiness. She noticed that I was steering clear of her, and so she began to direct some of her spite at me.

Many is the evening I quitted that office with a scalded heart and a feeling of depression at her unprovoked malice.

I had been in London six months now and seemed no closer to getting a home together for myself and the twins.

Chapter 34

LONDON WAS HARD TO navigate. It turned out graduates were cheap to come by, and the jobs I seemed able to get quickly were quite poorly paid. However, London had one massive advantage over Mulhouse, it was only a cheap Ryanair flight away from Dublin.

Sonja met me off the airport bus and we went straight to Bewleys. It was a sunny day in June and Grafton Street was full of cheerful girls in bright colours. My heart was light, light, for the first time in months. I was so happy to be back in Dublin.

Inside we queued and chatted.

"You look really well," she said. But added, "Maybe the hair's a bit too short."

I looked at her. As usual, her face was perfect. Not a single spot. "Why are you wearing those funny trainers?" I asked her.

"They're comfortable," she said. She was doing a part-time waitressing job. "I need a glass of wine." So she got a white wine and I had a milky Bewleys' coffee.

I drank my coffee and relaxed back into my seat. Sonja lit a cigarette and took a sip from her wine. It was so chilled that little drops of condensation collected on it, like dew.

She took me back to the little flat in Rathmines that she and Brian shared. One bedroom, a living room with a little kitchenette off it. The bathroom was downstairs. They shared it with the inhabitant of the other flat, an out-of-work nurse. She was very friendly and cleaned the bathroom every day. If you wanted a hot bath you had to put fifty pence pieces in the meter.

They didn't share a bedroom. Brian lived in the bedroom, and Sonja slept on the sofa bed in the living room.

"I just can't stand his mess," she said, by way of explanation.

We stuffed my suitcase behind the sofa and made tea.

Brian came in, beaming and full of plans as always.

"Hiya Anna!" he said. "How's life in France and London? How are the twins?"

At least back in Dublin among people who knew my past I could talk openly about my children. In London I never mention my situation. I can't face the reactions, the judgements.

We talked and talked and ate and watched TV. Brian went off to sleep in his messy bedroom and Sonja generously gave me the pull-out sofa while she slept on the floor on a roll-out mattress. I undressed quickly in the chilly room and threw my clothes over the back of the armchair. We slept and slept till Brian came in to get some breakfast the next morning.

He pulled back the curtains and I opened my eyes. I felt relief. For the first time in months, I was waking up in the right place. His eyes rested briefly on my untidy heap of clothes. There was a silky bra and a camisole on top of the pile. He picked up the camisole and whistled. "This yours, Anna?"

Then he went into the kitchenette and made us all tea. He brought it to us as we lay in bed, and when he'd gone, Sonja got up and started to dress. Grabbing my bra off the back of the chair where it lay she flung it at me muttering "seductive bitch!" I burst out laughing. Brian was like a brother to me.

An hour later, Brian had gone out but we were still in the flat. Sonja had been weighing herself, applying mascara, and pouting in the mirror as she applied her make-up. She had managed to get herself a few hours as an artists' model down at the Irish Academy of Art to supplement her wages from waitressing and was very anxious about her appearance. I noticed that although she still looked great, a lot of her old confidence had gone, and she seemed troubled and resentful. There was an atmosphere, a tension, as if she found my visit burdensome. It was clear my friends were finding postgraduate life difficult. Brian had no job and relied on Unemployment Benefit and odd-jobs and Sonja was waitressing and posing as an artists' model.

I could also see that Sonja and Brian's relationship was not making either of them happy.

"I know!" I said brightly. "Why don't you show me what Brian's lair is really like?"

We crept guiltily into his room and tiptoed round it, holding our noses, and giggling more and more.

"God, it's bad!" I picked up a smelly sock and threw it at Sonja who ducked and darted away from it. Dirty underwear and grey t-shirts lay in little piles all over the floor. Bits of Brian's writing were scattered everywhere, and his bed, obviously never made, was an uninviting tangle of grey sheets. There were no pillowcases on the pillows and a little feather fluttered around as we moved about. I was standing over his desk now and fingering the crisp A4 paper in the typewriter.

"Don't touch his writing," said Sonja quickly. She moved forward and pushed my hand away.

"Okay," I said, sulkily. Stepping backwards, I tripped over a book on Irish History that was lying on the floor and landed on my bum. The two of us were laughing now.

"Observe the male artist in his workshop!" I said,

"Oh yes," agreed Sonja, "The genius at his work!"

"Do you think he'll ever manage to finish anything?" I asked her. She just shrugged.

"Don't you sleep with him anymore?" I asked her. I knew that back in Germany her mum had sorted her out with the pill.

"Yes, sometimes. I come in here for that," she said.

Then we crept out, closing the door behind us. Brian would kill us if he knew.

We walked into town and I suggested we look for jobs.

"Everything would be better if we only had decent money!" I told Sonja. She agreed. Her mother was constantly pressuring her to give up on Dublin and come home to Germany.

So we went to FÁS, the employment agency, and studied the little cards with job details on. There wasn't much going on, and the wages were lower than what I was earning in London.

We got tired and went to our old haunt, O'Neill's in Suffolk Street. We sat in the comfortable gloom and I looked around me. I was relieved to see that nothing had changed. From where we sat everyone who entered could be seen.

It was early in the day and the atmosphere was subdued. The pub, freshly cleaned, prepared for another day, and the barmen, in their black trousers and white shirts were busy behind the bar, unstacking glasses, and cleaning taps. The clink of glasses was muffled and somehow restrained, but all the promise of another good day, another good night, was in those sounds.

We ordered two glasses of Guinness and sat while they were prepared. In London, I had been shocked to see when you ordered Guinness they poured it straight into the glass, right to the top, without setting it aside for a few minutes to allow the liquid to settle properly, and then topping up the head.

Now I sipped my drink with pleasure, the perfect head on it made it look so compact and appetising. It tasted better too.

With our drinks in our hands, we could relax, sit back, watch and listen. Around the other side of the pub was where Kielty used to sit, holding court. One evening he sat setting fire to twenty-pound notes to show how little regard he had for money. There was no sign of him now. According to Sonja, he had given up the drink. Kielty minus the drink was difficult to imagine. I wondered sadly if he ever thought of me nowadays.

When we got back to the flat in Rathmines, it was time for tea but there was nothing to eat. I looked in the kitchen. A couple of mouldy potatoes and a tin of beans was all I could find. We were miles from a decent supermarket and we didn't have access to a car. Sonja slumped in an armchair, despondent. We were waiting for Brian to come in.

Soon he appeared and at once the energy in the room changed. "What's up, girls?" he asked. "You look gloomy! Have you been to a funeral?"

"No funeral," I said, "Just FÁS...!"

Brian laughed. "Oh right," he said. "That IS depressing all right...."

Sonja was weeping quietly and Brian immediately went over to where she sat. He knelt down by her and gently pulled back her curtain of hair.

"Sonja! What's wrong?"

Sonja said she didn't know. Brian stood up and looked at us both.

"We need to eat," he said decisively. The three of us pooled our money, so Brian could tackle some shopping on Upper Rathmines Road.

"Tell me what you would like," he told us. Sonja began to rhapsodise: "Prawn cocktail, with fresh lemon, chicken in wine sauce and chocolate pudding for afters...."

"....and fresh cream!" I added. Brian looked doubtfully at the money we had pooled. Then a determined look came over his face.

"Don't worry, girls," he said. "I'll be back soon with everything your hearts desire!" Then he was gone.

As soon as he'd left I asked Sonja why she had been crying.

"I dunno," she said, "I just didn't think it would be like this after we graduated."

I knew how she felt. During our years at Trinity we had done without money, but had thought some miracle would deliver us great wages once we had our degrees.

After an hour Brian returned. He was wearing a pleased, satisfied look. He was carrying a plastic bag half full of groceries which he rapidly unpacked before our eyes; milk, bread, potatoes, chicken breasts.

Then he unzipped his padded jacket and triumphantly produced a bottle of wine, fresh prawns, a lemon and three chocolate puddings. Sonja and I were stunned and amazed. We hurried to assemble the food and get it into the kitchen. We were in awe of Brian. We knew the money we had given him could not have covered it and that he had resorted to shop-lifting. But somehow we didn't feel guilty. The meal and the wine would cheer us up, make us feel less cheated.

That night, as I drifted off to sleep, I faced the awful fact that it would be too difficult to bring the twins back to Dublin. I would have to stick it out in England and try to come up with a plan. My heart was very still and quiet as I assimilated this unpalatable fact.

Soon, the time came for me to say goodbye to my friends and get my Ryanair flight back to London.

Chapter 35

NOT LONG AFTER I was back in London, I bumped into my cousin Emer. In one of those unbelievable coincidences, I actually bumped into my cousin in London, a city of nine million or whatever it is. I was on one of my lunch breaks, and I wandered into one of those Balls Brothers pubs that were everywhere in the city in the 80s, and there was Emer, her black hair flying as she darted about behind the bar, serving the throngs of noisy office workers.

She wasn't particularly pleased to see me. We'd never had much in common apart from our holidays together as children, but we met up a week later at Elephant and Castle, both latching on to each other in this hostile landscape.

As I came out of the tube at Elephant and Castle and looked around, I felt amazed that here was somewhere even grubbier and more dismal than Clapham. I went over to Emer who was waiting for me.

"So, where's the elephant? or the castle?" These places never lived up to their fabulous names.

We went to a steamy little café where we chain-smoked and stared out the windows at the terrible dereliction about us.

"Sinead O'Connor lives somewhere round here," Emer mused.

I gazed at her in wonderment "Why?" I asked.

We decided to go to the local cinema. It looked like the cinema that time forgot but Emer insisted.

"We're going," she said. "It'll pass the time. It's warmer than out here in the freezing cold, and they don't care if you smoke."

We bought our tickets and went in. The place was so damp it would have taken a lot of cigarettes to make it light up.

As far as I can remember, we were the only two people in the place. The seats were faded and threadbare, with their shabby red velvet, and a smell of must. We sat through the movie while Emer puffed energetically on her fags and I huddled next to her in my coat.

We talked about Dublin, about who had managed to get a job and stay on, and who had been forced to come to London like us. I told her I'd been to FÁS. Emer looked at me and asked "Waste of time? No real jobs?" I admitted she was right.

"By the way," I mused, "what does FÁS mean?"

Emer laughed ruefully. "Ah yes, FÁS! It's Irish for "Development."

Neither of us admitted that we felt like fish out of water here in London.

I told Emer about my landlady and the four noisy little dogs. She told me her landlady was a chain smoker, and a skinflint to boot.

"Honestly," she said. "It's gas! Why don't you come back with me now, and I show it to you. It's a real dive!"

I looked at my watch. A long Saturday alone stretched ahead of me and I didn't have any better offers. Emer was entertaining company so I agreed to catch the tube back to Islington with her.

The house where she had her bedsit lived up to her glum description. My own digs were not great, but at least the house was used as a family home. It had a proper sitting room, and a clean kitchen, and that convivial atmosphere that you associate with a place where people who genuinely care about each other live. Emer's abode had no such pretensions. As we opened the heavy Victorian front door, a strong musty smell assailed me. The door banged behind us and Emer swore out loud, "Shit! She still hasn't replaced the light bulb so there's no bloody light in the hall."

Together we clambered up the dark staircase. We went up two flights of stairs and passed at least two other doors before Emer stopped in front of another one and started poking at the lock with her key.

In the gloom I could make out the shape of a public phone on the wall. "I see you have your own private phone," I said.

Until I came to London, I had never seen ones like this. They were really old-fashioned black things with A and B painted in white on them. You put your money in and then when you got a tone you had to quickly press B. What a carry on. When she succeeded in opening it, we both toppled into her little room.

Emer is a bit of a free spirit – there weren't many possessions around. I sat on the bed and was impressed by its springiness. The wallpaper must have dated from the 60s, and the curtains were an interesting shade of brown with big orange circles on them. A few dog-eared paperbacks lay on the window sill and two big art books lay on the battered desk in the corner. I could see that Emer was trying to continue with her art as a big sketch pad lay open on the floor. I wondered if she was still doing heroin. She had taken up chasing the dragon in Dublin while she was still an undergraduate.

I asked her if she had any beer.

"We'll go down to the kitchen now and see what there is," she replied.

We got out of the little room and proceeded cautiously back down the narrow staircase. One floor down Emer stopped and pushed open a narrow door. "This is the kitchen," she announced.

I looked around and saw that the small kitchen had washing machines lined all the way around its circumference.

"Why does the landlady keep all these old washing machines in here?" I asked in amazement. Emer laughed. "She's a miser. I told you. She can't bear to throw anything away. She thinks someday she'll find someone who can fix them, and then she'll make money!"

"Christ! Does she have mental issues?"

Emer shrugged. "Who doesn't?"

She had opened the communal fridge and was peering into it. At last she gave a grunt of satisfaction and pulled out two cans of Carlsberg.

"Probably the Best Lager in the World......," she quipped in a throaty bass.

I laughed.

We ran back up to her room and began to drink. She put the telly on but the picture was grainy and kept dissolving into zig zags.

About half an hour later, there were steps outside and someone rapped loudly on the door. Emer squeezed my arm and motioned to me to be very still. But it was no good. A man's angry voice penetrated the gloom.

"I know you're in there! You taking my beers again – you thieving little Irish bitch!" One final thump on the door and the steps retreated noisily back down the stairs.

"The natives are friendly, aren't they?" I whispered. Still, we shouldn't have nicked his beers.

We sat there whispering to each other for a while but in the end, our boredom overcame our fear.

We pooled our money. We had 15 pounds and 37 pence in total.

"That's enough for us to get langered," said Emer with satisfaction. "I'll take you to my local. But first, we have to get dressed up."

She guided me up the stairs this time, and when we reached the very top of the building she paused outside the door and lent her ear against it. After a minute she called softly, "Gladys, are you there, Gladys?"

Gladys was the landlady's name.

"I better introduce you in case you end up staying the night," she said.

However, Gladys didn't come to the door. Gently, Emer lent against it and pushed it open. The room was an Aladdin's cave. I followed her in and looked around. The place was crammed full with wardrobes, stacks of magazines, and books. Two big boxes were full of old vinyl records, and there were hats and boots in abundance. Emer opened one of the wardrobes and I sneezed at the dust. She began to pull out items.

"This will look great on me, and this on you.... Here, take this......"

They were nylon clothes in garish colours from the 70s. The two of us dressed up like mad hippies. Emer was in luminous green flares and pink jacket, and I was in a purple maxi dress and big black platform boots. We found a wig for her and huge sunglasses for me. Then we draped ourselves in beads and grabbed an old guitar from the corner. We looked at our reflections in the spotty old mirror on the wardrobe door and laughed at ourselves. Then we retreated down the stairs and out into the cold night air of Islington.

We caused a bit of a stir at the pub.

"Where's the party, girls?" they asked.

"It's by invitation only, sorry!" replied Emer. She was in her element. There was a group of young men at the bar, they watched as she ordered our pints.

"Drinks all round!" she said to the barman, adding, "Only joking!"

The fellows laughed obligingly and soon invited us to join them in a game of pool. I felt happy inside the pub. Not that it was anything special – but I always get a sense of comfort from being inside a pub. It was just the usual assortment of people, but we all had something in common; we were all fugitives from reality.

Emer was impressing the lads with her pool ability. One of the men, a stocky chap called Larry, seemed to take a particular shine to her.

"Where you from?" he asked.

"Dublin's fair city!" we replied, and he began to sing, "...where the girls are so pretty! What're you called?"

"I'm Molly, and she's Malone," quipped Emer. She wasn't giving anything away. I sensed Larry's mood hardening slightly.

"Stuck up, aren't you?" he said. But he soon bought us a round and so we made up to him a bit, praising him and making him think he was great. His mates hung around the bar, and I could tell they were sizing up Emer's backside when she was leaning over the pool table to cue. I began to feel uneasy. When she went to the Ladies I followed her.

"Listen, I think they might be expecting something for the drinks," I said. "From now on, let's buy our own."

"Oh, you mean sex," said Emer disdainfully. "Yeh, they're all mad for it over here, all the time. Must be something in the water...but look, they're alright. Let's get a few drinks out of them and then we'll scarper." For the rest of the time, I felt uneasy, like we were in the middle of a big misunderstanding. When Larry pinched Emer on the bum she reared up at him. I knew she wasn't interested in him and despite the fact that she always attracted men, I think she preferred women.

"Fuck off!" she told him.

He didn't like that and it began to get nasty. I hastily backed off and grabbed the useless guitar. I'd tried to play and then realised it had only two strings. "Come on," I said. "Let's get outta here."

We got away from them and made a beeline through the streets to the safety of Emer's bedsit. As she struggled with the lock she said, "never mind, maybe there'll be something good on telly."

Chapter 36

WORKING IN LONDON WAS an experience. On Friday nights, there was a special kind of energy in the air as thousands of pent-up office workers were released into the bars; a prelude to their forty-eight hours of weekend freedom.

In the bar, I met a bunch of Australians. One of them caught my eye. He was slender and his hair was that unusual shade of pale red that is always worth a second glance. He laughed frequently at people's jokes, but though he seemed at home in the crowd, there was something different about him, and he held himself slightly aloof as if to say, "Don't come too close for I am special."

His name was Graeme and he was from Adelaide. He made it clear to me that this was a cut above Sydney. I was happy to believe him. I liked his quick elegant movements and his bright intelligence. We struck up a rapport and began seeing each other. He shared a beautiful flat with some other young Australians in Ladbroke Grove. I didn't tell him about Ireland, or about the baby daughters I had left behind in France. I felt that he was a secretive person and didn't need to know everything. Then one day we were in the Underground, and there was the unusual sight of a toddler in a pushchair. We both looked at the child, and then at each other. I felt a pang at the thought of my own children, he was smiling.

"Maybe one day," he said and laughed. I thought it was only natural he should want a child of his own one day. Suddenly it seemed like the right time to tell him. We had spent a lovely day together and I was feeling close to him.

As we hurried down the Underground escalators I told him I had twins. At first, he didn't hear me. My words were swallowed up by the din of a passing tube rattling by. When I repeated myself, his eyes darkened and he turned a stony profile to me. My heart sank. We got on the tube and sat together in silence. I waited for three stops before I said anything. I felt discouraged and apprehensive. At last, I spoke.

"What are you thinking?" I asked him. "I'm thinking what a silly bitch you are." he said. My heart sank. He then proceeded to lecture me about the importance of contraception and the terrors and pitfalls of growing up without a father. As I listened to him droning on, my grief turned to anger.

"Oh, fuck off," I said. "You know nothing about it."

I longed to get away from him but where could I go? Back to my gloomy little bedsit? I turned away and thought about the cold winter city I was in. I wanted to weep. I hated London at night, the gloomy half-light that covered the mean little 24-hour shops and the endless, endless rows of tiny terraced houses and faceless passers-by and endless cars. I couldn't break up with him now, I couldn't bear to be alone tonight.

The enormity and loneliness of London overwhelmed me – it was hard to keep my life-light alive in this pressing multitude, hard to hang on to the conviction that I mattered, that my tiny life mattered.

Everywhere there were teeming masses of people that I would never know or even see a second time. I was being swallowed up. I felt so alone and quite frightened. When I thought of my bedsit in Clapham, when I thought of huge

Clapham Common, the monotony of my 9 to 5 job, and my babies so far away, a dark pit opened up inside of me, as if I were going to fall into it. I reached for Graeme's hand. He didn't squeeze it but at least he didn't pull it away from me.

It was Saturday, and I thought of the evening ahead. There was something dreadful about spending Saturday night all alone, something that proclaimed you were irredeemably cast out. How much pleasanter to spend the night with Graeme in his spacious house-share, than to return alone to my bedsit. There would be food, for Graeme could cook, and there would be wine and later there might be bed and closeness. Yes, there was at least that comfort to look forward to.

With relief, I saw that we were turning the corner into his street, the big white face of the house offered a welcome touch of reassurance to my evening. Now in companionable silence, we struggled up the narrow stairs with our shopping bags. In a moment we were inside the big bright kitchen and there were other people there to talk to. Someone poured me a glass of wine and I chatted and enthused. For tonight at least, I was safe.

Later, in bed, he asked me if I was on the pill. I said no. He sighed. He told me he knew what the Irish were like because he went out with one for six months, and she was hung up about contraception too. I was silent. I felt stupid.

He got up then, to go to the loo. I lay in the bed and felt warm for the first time that day, yes, warm and relaxed. The room was large and comfortable compared to my bedsit. There were a few books about photography on a small shelf next to the bed and a big black and white poster on the far wall. I was surprised that it was an erotic type of photo of a young man.

I was glad when Graeme climbed back in the bed beside me and I could feel the warm weight of him. For a while, I lay with my eyes closed and listened to the sounds of traffic and sirens. As I drifted off to sleep, it all became muffled.

****

The next morning we are in the kitchen, Graeme stands with his back to me, fumbling in a drawer for cutlery. The radio is on. There's a big window, and I look out at the houses on the opposite side of the street. The windows are like big empty eyes, staring vacantly back at me. The trees tremble in the wind, they don't have many leaves left now, for autumn has come suddenly.

I drink the tea that Graeme has made for me. I drink slowly because I know that we will not spend the day together and that I will end up having to return to my bedsit and spend the rest of the weekend alone.

He joins me at the big pine table. "Is there enough sugar in it?" he asks.

He doesn't look at me. "Yes, it's fine," I reply. I can't think of anything to say. If I ask him what his plans are, it will sound as though I am fishing for an invitation.

Into the silence comes one of his housemates, Matilda. She is a plump, tanned girl with shoulder-length brown hair and a presence that radiates self-confidence.

"Hiya," she says to us. "What are you up to today?"

Neither Graeme nor I say anything, and she just shrugs and goes on making herself a drink. The two of them exchange comments about the meal last night. Then, at last, she drifts off and Graeme and I are left together again.

There is a pause, and then I fill the emptiness with the words, "Will you walk me to the tube? I think I'd better get back." I make the words sound airy and light.

As we walk to the tube I feel the ache of our impending farewell. I buy my ticket and turn to Graeme. The obligatory exchange of kisses and soon I am on the tube. I gaze wearily out at the billboards and rows of piece-meal houses. This is the Big Smoke. I harbour no illusions about Graeme. I know we will probably not see each other again. When I get out at my stop I climb slowly up the steps to the exit. A strong gust of dusty air rushes past me as the tube pulls out. I exit into the unlovely streets of this neighbourhood where I have lived for six months and which I will never call home. I walk back to my bedsit feeling the familiar dread and decide I can't go back yet. There's a pub on the other side of the street called 'O'Donovan and Sons'. Oh, come out, come out, O'Donovan or one of your sons, and speak to me! I am so homesick I could cry. I cross over to the pub and get half a lager.

How I wish I was a Trinity student again! Young and intact with nothing to weigh me down except the canvas bag over my shoulder containing my beloved books, and my notebook full of my thoughts and exciting hopes about my future. I begin to weep silently. I feel so old and worn-out inside. It's as though a terrible schism has occurred, separating me from my own life, as though I have unknowingly crossed some wide river, and now I am standing on the wrong side of it with no way of getting back to where my real life is. I feel like a ghost. I am separated from my babies, my books, Dublin, my very self.

When I have finished my drink I get up and walk slowly back to my bedsit.

About the Author

PATRICIA BURGESS-MCCORMICK WAS BORN in Northern Ireland and educated in Northern Ireland, Switzerland, Luxembourg and England. She attended Trinity College, Dublin and graduated in 1986.

She has worked as a teacher, translator and NHS administrator.

She lives in Sussex with her partner Mike and her family.

She is an avid reader and supporter of local theatre.

Lightning Source UK Ltd.
Milton Keynes UK
UKHW010936070322
399687UK00002B/367